R.W Taylor, Sir Walter Scott

Scott's Poems

The Lady of the Lake part III cantos V & VI

R.W Taylor, Sir Walter Scott

Scott's Poems
The Lady of the Lake part III cantos V & VI

ISBN/EAN: 9783337123178

Printed in Europe, USA, Canada, Australia, Japan

Cover: Foto ©Andreas Hilbeck / pixelio.de

More available books at **www.hansebooks.com**

SCOTT'S POEMS

HE LADY OF THE LAKE

*WITH INTRODUCTION, NOTES, AND
GLOSSARIAL INDEX,*

BY

R. W. TAYLOR, M. A.,

ASSISTANT-MASTER IN RUGBY SCHOOL; AND FORMERLY
FELLOW OF ST. JOHN'S COLLEGE, CAMBRIDGE.

PART III.
CANTOS V. & VI.

TORONTO:
ADAM MILLER & CO.,
1879.

THE LADY OF THE LAKE.

CANTO FIFTH.

𝕿𝖍𝖊 𝕮𝖔𝖒𝖇𝖆𝖙.

I.

FAIR as the earliest beam of eastern light,
When first, by the bewildered pilgrim spied,
It smiles upon the dreary brow of night,
  And silvers o'er the torrent's foaming tide,
And lights the fearful path on mountain side ;—
  Fair as that beam, although the fairest far,
Giving to horror grace, to danger pride,
  Shine martial Faith, and Courtesy's bright star,
Through all the wreckful storms that cloud the brow of
    War.

II.

  That early beam, so fair and sheen,
  Was twinkling through the hazel screen,
  When, rousing at its glimmer red,
  The warriors left their lowly bed,
  Looked out upon the dappled sky,
  Muttered their soldier matins by,
  And then awaked their fire, to steal,
  As short and rude, their soldier meal.
  That o'er, the Gael around him threw
  His graceful plaid of varied hue,
  And, true to promise, led the way,
  By thicket green and mountain gray.

M 2]

A wildering path !—they winded now
Along the precipice's brow,
Commanding the rich scenes beneath,
The windings of the Forth and Teith,
And all the vales between that lie,
Till Stirling's turrets melt in sky;
Then, sunk in copse, their farthest glance
Gained not the length of horseman's lance.
'Twas oft so steep, the foot was fain
Assistance from the hand to gain ;
So tangled oft, that, bursting through,
Each hawthorn shed her showers of dew—
That diamond dew, so pure and clear,
It rivals all but Beauty's tear !

III.

At length they came where, stern and steep,
The hill sinks down upon the deep.
Here Vennachar in silver flows,
There, ridge on ridge, Benledi rose ;
Ever the hollow path twined on,
Beneath steep bank and threatening stone ;
An hundred men might hold the post
With hardihood against a host.
The rugged mountain's scanty cloak
Was dwarfish shrubs of birch and oak,
With shingles bare, and cliffs between,
And patches bright of bracken green,
And heather black, that waved so high,
It held the copse in rivalry.
But where the lake slept deep and still,
Dank osiers fringed the swamp and hill ;
And oft both path and hill were torn,
Where wintry torrents down had borne,
And heaped upon the cumbered land
Its wreck of gravel, rocks, and sand.
So toilsome was the road to trace,
The guide, abating of his pace,
Led slowly through the pass's jaws,
And asked Fitz-James, by what strange cause
He sought these wilds, traversed by few,
Without a pass from Roderick Dhu.

IV.

' Brave Gael, my pass, in danger tried,
Hangs in my belt, and by my side ;
Yet, sooth to tell,' the Saxon said,
' I dreamt not now to claim its aid.
When here, but three days since, I came,
Bewildered in pursuit of game,
All seemed as peaceful and as still
As the mist slumbering on yon hill ;
Thy dangerous Chief was then afar,
Nor soon expected back from war.
Thus said, at least, my mountain-guide,
Though deep perchance the villain lied.'—
' Yet why a second venture try ?'—
' A warrior thou, and ask me why !—
Moves our free course by such fixed cause,
As gives the poor mechanic laws ?
Enough, I sought to drive away
The lazy hours of peaceful day ;
Slight cause will then suffice to guide
A Knight's free footsteps far and wide—
A falcon flown, a greyhound strayed,
The merry glance of mountain maid :
Or, if a path be dangerous known,
The danger's self is lure alone.' —

V.

' Thy secret keep, I urge thee not ;—
Yet, ere again ye sought this spot,·
Say, heard ye nought of Lowland war,
Against Clan-Alpine, raised by Mar ?'
—' No, by my word ;—of bands prepared
To guard King James's sports I heard ;
Nor doubt I aught, but, when they hear
This muster of the mountaineer,
Their pennons will abroad be flung,
Which else in Doune had peaceful hung.'—
' Free be they flung ! for we were loth
Their silken folds should feast the moth.
Free be they flung !—as free shall wave
Clan-Alpine's pine in banner brave.

But, Stranger, peaceful since you came,
Bewildered in the mountain game,
Whence the bold boast by which you shew
Vich-Alpine's vowed and mortal foe?
'Warrior, but yester-morn, I knew
Nought of thy Chieftain, Roderick Dhu,
Save as an outlawed desperate man,
The chief of a rebellious clan,
Who, in the Regent's court and sight,
With ruffian dagger stabbed a knight :
Yet this alone might from his part
Sever each true and loyal heart.'

VI.

Wrothful at such arraignment foul,
Dark lowered the clansman's sable scowl.
A space he paused, then sternly said,
'And heard'st thou why he drew his blade?
Heard'st thou that shameful word and blow
Brought Roderick's vengeance on his foe?
What recked the Chieftain if he stood
On Highland heath or Holy-Rood?
He rights such wrong where it is given,
If it were in the court of heaven.'
'Still was it outrage;—yet, 'tis true,
Not then claimed sovereignty his due;
While Albany, with feeble hand,
Held borrowed truncheon of command,
The young King, mewed in Stirling tower,
Was stranger to respect and power.
But then, thy Chieftain's robber life !
Winning mean prey by causeless strife,
Wrenching from ruined Lowland swain
His herds and harvest reared in vain.
Methinks a soul like thine should scorn
The spoils from such foul foray borne.'

VII.

The Gael beheld him grim the while,
And answered with disdainful smile—
'Saxon, from yonder mountain high,
I marked thee send delighted eye,

Far to the south and east, where lay,
Extended in succession gay,
Deep waving fields and pastures green,
With gentle slopes and groves between :—
These fertile plains, that softened vale,
Were once the birthright of the Gael;
The stranger came with iron hand,
And from our fathers reft the land.
Where dwell we now?   See, rudely swell
Crag over crag, and fell o'er fell.
Ask we this savage hill we tread,   .
For fattened steer or household bread;
Ask we for flocks these shingles dry,
And well the mountain might reply—
" To you, as to your sires of yore,
Belong the target and claymore !
I give you shelter in my breast,
Your own good blades must win the rest."
Pent in this fortress of the North,
Think'st thou we will not sally forth,
To spoil the spoiler as we may,
And from the robber rend the prey?
Ay, by my soul !—While on yon plain
The Saxon rears one shock of grain ;
While, of ten thousand herds, there strays
But one along yon river's maze—
The Gael, of plain and river heir,
Shall, with strong hand, redeem his share.
Where live the mountain Chiefs who hold
That plundering,Lowland field and fold
Is aught but retribution true?
Seek other cause 'gainst Roderick Dhu.'

VIII.

Answered Fitz-James—' And, if I sought,
Think'st thou no other could be brought?
What deem ye of my path waylaid?
My life given o'er to ambuscade?'—
' As of a meed to rashness due:
Hadst thou sent warning fair and true—
I seek my hound, or falcon strayed,
I seek, good faith, a Highland maid—

Free hadst thou been to come and go;
But secret path marks secret foe.
Nor yet, for this, even as a spy,
Hadst thou, unheard, been doomed to die,
Save to fulfil an augury.'
'Well, let it pass; nor will I now
Fresh cause of enmity avow,
To chafe thy mood and cloud thy brow.
Enough, I am by promise tied
To match me with this man of pride:
Twice have I sought Clan-Alpine's glen
In peace; but when I come agen,
I come with banner, brand, and bow,
As leader seeks his mortal foe.
For love-lorn swain, in lady's bower,
Ne'er panted for the appointed hour,
As I, until before me stand
This rebel Chieftain and his band!'

IX.

'Have, then, thy wish!'—he whistled shrill,
And he was answered from the hill;
Wild as the scream of the curlew,
From crag to crag the signal flew.
Instant, through copse and heath, arose
Bonnets, and spears, and bended bows;
On right, on left, above, below,
Sprung up at once the lurking foe;
From shingles gray their lances start,
The bracken bush sends forth the dart,
The rushes and the willow-wand
Are bristling into axe and brand,
And every tuft of broom gives life
To plaided warrior armed for strife.
That whistle garrisoned the glen
At once with full five hundred men,
As if the yawning hill to heaven
A subterranean host had given.
Watching their leader's beck and will,
All silent there they stood, and still.
Like the loose crags whose threatening mass
Lay tottering o'er the hollow pass,

As if an infant's touch could urge
Their headlong passage down the verge,
With step and weapon forward flung,
Upon the mountain-side they hung.
The Mountaineer cast glance of pride
Along Benledi's living side,
Then fixed his eye and sable brow
Full on Fitz-James—'How say'st thou now?
These are Clan-Alpine's warriors true;
And, Saxon—I am Roderick Dhu!'

X.

Fitz-James was brave:—Though to his heart
The life-blood thrilled with sudden start,
He manned himself with dauntless air,
Returned the Chief his haughty stare,
His back against a rock he bore,
And firmly placed his foot before :—
'Come one, come all! this rock shall fly
From its firm base as soon as I.'
Sir Roderick marked—and in his eyes
Respect was mingled with surprise,
And the stern joy which warriors feel
In foemen worthy of their steel.
Short space he stood—then waved his hand:
Down sunk the disappearing band;
Each warrior vanished where he stood,
In broom or bracken, heath or wood;
Sunk brand, and spear, and bended bow,
In osiers pale and copses low;
It seemed as if their mother Earth
Had swallowed up her warlike birth.
The wind's last breath had tossed in air,
Pennon, and plaid, and plumage fair—
The next but swept a lone hill-side,
Where heath and fern were waving wide :
The sun's last glance was glinted back,
From spear and glaive, from targe and jack—
The next, all unreflected, shone
On bracken green, and cold gray stone.

XI.

Fitz-James looked round—yet scarce believed
The witness that his sight received ;
Such appari.ion well might seem
Delusion of a dreadful dream.
Sir Roderick in suspense he eyed,
And to his look the Chief replied,
'Fear nought—nay, that I need not say—
But—doubt not aught from mine array.
Thou art my guest ;—I pledged my word
As far as Coilantogle ford :
Nor would I call a clansman's brand
For aid against one valiant hand,
Though on our strife lay every vale
Rent by the Saxon from the Gael.
So move we on ;—I only meant
To shew the reed on which you leant,
Deeming this path you might pursue
Without a pass from Roderick Dhu.'
They moved ;—I said Fitz-James was brave,
As ever knight that belted glaive ;
Yet dare not say, that now his blood
Kept on its wont and tempered flood,
As, following Roderick's stride, he drew
That seeming lonesome pathway through,
Which yet, by fearful proof, was rife
With lances, that, to take his life,
Waited but signal from a guide,
So late dishonoured and defied.
Ever, by stealth, his eye sought round
The vanished guardians of the ground,
And still, from copse and heather deep,
Fancy saw spear and broadsword peep,
And in the plover's shrilly strain,
The signal whistle heard again.
Nor breathed he free till far behind
The pass was left ; for then they wind
Along a wide and level green,
Where neither tree nor tuft was seen,
Nor rush nor bush of broom was near,
To hide a bonnet or a spear.

XII.

The Chief in silence strode before,
And reached that torrent's sounding shore,
Which, daughter of three mighty lakes,
From Vennachar in silver breaks,
Sweeps through the plain, and ceaseless mines
On Bochastle the mouldering lines,
Where Rome, the Empress of the world,
Of yore her eagle wings unfurled :
And here his course the Chieftain staid,
Threw down his target and his plaid,
And to the Lowland warrior said :—
'Bold Saxon ! to his promise just,
Vich-Alpine has discharged his trust.
This murderous Chief, this ruthless man,
This head of a rebellious clan,
Hath led thee safe, through watch and ward,
Far past Clan-Alpine's outmost guard.
Now, man to man, and steel to steel,
A Chieftain's vengeance thou shalt feel.
See, here, all vantageless I stand,
Armed, like thyself, with single brand,:
For this is Coilantogle ford,
And thou must keep thee with thy sword.'

XIII.

The Saxon paused :—' I ne'er delayed,
When foeman bade me draw my blade ;
Nay more, brave Chief, I vowed thy death :
Yet sure thy fair and generous faith,
And my deep debt for life preserved,
A better meed have well deserved :
Can nought but blood our feud atone ?
Are there no means ?'—' No, Stranger, none !
And hear—to fire thy flagging zeal—
The Saxon cause rests on thy steel :
For thus spoke Fate, by prophet bred
Between the living and the dead ;
"Who spills the foremost foeman's life,
His party conquers in the strife."
'Then, by my word,' the Saxon said,
'Thy riddle is already read.

Seek yonder brake beneath the cliff—
There lies Red Murdoch, stark and stiff.
Thus Fate has solved her prophecy,
Then yield to Fate, and not to me.
To James, at Stirling, let us go,
When, if thou wilt be still his foe,
Or if the King shall not agree
To grant thee grace and favour free,
I plight mine honour, oath, and word,
That, to thy native strengths restored,
With each advantage shalt thou stand,
That aids thee now to guard thy land.'

XIV.

Dark lightning flashed from Roderick's eye—
'Soars thy presumption, then, so high,
Because a wretched kern ye slew,
Homage to name to Roderick Dhu?
He yields not, he, to man nor Fate!
Thou add'st but fuel to my hate :—
My clansman's blood demands revenge.—
Not yet prepared ?—By heaven, I change
My thought, and hold thy valour light
As that of some vain carpet knight,
Who ill deserved my courteous care,
And whose best boast is but to wear
A braid of his fair lady's hair.'—
—' I thank thee, Roderick, for the word!
It nerves my heart, it steels my sword;
For I have sworn this braid to stain
In the best blood that warms thy vein.
Now, truce, farewell! and, ruth, begone!
Yet think not that by thee alone,
Proud Chief! can courtesy be shewn;
Though not from copse, or heath, or cairn,
Start at my whistle clansmen stern,
Of this small horn one feeble blast
Would fearful odds against thee cast.
But fear not—doubt not—which thou wilt—
We try this quarrel hilt to hilt.'
Then each at once his falchion drew,
Each on the ground his scabbard threw,

Now, gallant Saxon, hold thine own !
No maiden's hand is round thee thrown !
That desperate grasp thy frame might feel,
Through bars of brass and triple steel !—
They tug, they strain ! down, down they go,
The Gael above, Fitz-James below.
The Chieftain's gripe his throat compressed,
His knee was planted in his breast ;
His clotted locks he backward threw,
Across his brow his hand he drew,
From blood and mist to clear his sight,
Then gleamed aloft his dagger bright !—
—But hate and fury ill supplied
The stream of life's exhausted tide,
And all too late the advantage came,
To turn the odds of deadly game ;
For, while the dagger gleamed on high,
Reeled soul and sense, reeled brain and eye.
Down came the blow ! but in the heath
The erring blade found bloodless sheath.'
The struggling foe may now unclasp
The fainting Chief's relaxing grasp ;
Unwounded from the dreadful close,
But breathless all, Fitz-James arose.

XVII.

He faltered thanks to Heaven for life,
Redeemed, unhoped, from desperate strife ;
Next on his foe his look he cast,
Whose every gasp appeared his last ;
In Roderick's gore he dipped the braid—
' Poor Blanche ! thy wrongs are dearly paid ;
Yet with thy foe must die, or live,
The praise that Faith and Valour give.'
With that he blew a bugle note,
Undid the collar from his throat,
Unbonneted, and by the wave
Sat down his brow and hands to lave.
Then faint afar are heard the feet
Of rushing steeds in gallop fleet ;
The sounds increase, and now are seen
Four mounted squires in Lincoln green ;

XX.

The Douglas, who had bent his way
From Cambus-Kenneth's abbey gray,
Now, as he climbed the rocky shelf,
Held sad communion with himself:—
'Yes ! all is true my fears could frame;
A prisoner lies the noble Græme,
And fiery Roderick soon will feel
The vengeance of the royal steel.
I, only I, can ward their fate—
God grant the ransom come not late !
The Abbess hath her promise given,
My child shall be the bride of Heaven ;—
—Be pardoned one repining tear !
For He, who gave her, knows how dear,
How excellent ! but that is by,
And now my business is—to die.
—Ye towers ! within whose circuit dread
A Douglas by his sovereign bled ;
And thou, O sad and fatal mound !
That oft hast heard the death-axe sound,
As on the noblest of the land
Fell the stern headsman's bloody hand—
The dungeon, block, and nameless tomb,
Prepare—for Douglas seeks his doom !
—But hark ! what blithe and jolly peal
Makes the Franciscan steeple reel ?
And see ! upon the crowded street,
In motley groups what masquers meet !
Banner and pageant, pipe and drum,
And merry morrice-dancers come.
I guess, by all this quaint array,
The burghers hold their sports to-day.
James will be there ; he loves such show,
Where the good yeoman bends his bow,
And the tough wrestler foils his foe,
As well as where, in proud career,
The high-born tilter shivers spear.
I 'll follow to the Castle-park,
And play my prize ;—King James shall mark,
If age has tamed these sinews stark,
Whose force so oft, in happier days,
His boyish wonder loved to praise.'

N

XXI.

The Castle gates were open flung,
The quivering drawbridge rocked and rung,
And echoed loud the flinty street
Beneath the courser's clattering feet,
As slowly down the steep descent
Fair Scotland's King and nobles went,
While all along the crowded way
Was jubilee and loud huzza.
And ever James was bending low,
To his white jennet's saddlebow,
Doffing his cap to city dame,
Who smiled and blushed for pride and shame.
And well the simperer might be vain—
He chose the fairest of the train.
Gravely he greets each city sire,
Commends each pageant's quaint attire,
Gives to the dancers thanks aloud,
And smiles and nods upon the crowd,
Who rend the heavens with their acclaims,
' Long live the Commons' King, King James !'
Behind the King thronged peer and knight,
And noble dame and damsel bright,
Whose fiery steeds ill brooked the stay
Of the steep street and crowded way.
—But in the train you might discern
Dark lowering brow and visage stern ;
There nobles mourned their pride restrained,
And the mean burgher's joys disdained ;
And chiefs, who, hostage for their clan,
Were each from home a banished man,
There thought upon their own gray tower,
Their waving woods, their feudal power,
And deemed themselves a shameful part
Of pageant which they cursed in heart.

XXII.

Now, in the Castle-park, drew out
Their chequered bands the joyous rout.
There morricers, with bell at heel,
And blade in hand, their mazes wheel ;

But chief, beside the butts, there stand
Bold Robin Hood and all his band—
Friar Tuck with quarterstaff and cowl,
Old Scathelocke with his surly scowl.
Maid Marion, fair as ivory bone,
Scarlet, and Mutch, and Little John;
Their bugles challenge all that will,
In archery to prove their skill.
The Douglas bent a bow of might,
His first shaft centred in the white,
And when in turn he shot again,
His second split the first in twain.
From the King's hand must Douglas take
A silver dart, the archer's stake;
Fondly he watched, with watery eye,
Some answering glance of sympathy—
No kind emotion made reply !
Indifferent as to archer wight,
The monarch gave the arrow bright.

XXIII.

Now, clear the ring ! for, hand to hand,
The manly wrestlers take their stand.
Two o'er the rest superior rose,
And proud demanded mightier foes,
Nor called in vain; for Douglas came.
—For life is Hugh of Larbert lame;
Scarce better John of Alloa's fare,
Whom senseless home his comrades bear.
Prize of the wrestling match, the King
To Douglas gave a golden ring,
While coldly glanced his eye of blue,
As frozen drop of wintry dew.
Douglas would speak, but in his breast
His struggling soul his words suppressed;
Indignant then he turned him where
Their arms the brawny yeomen bare,
To hurl the massive bar in air.
When each his utmost strength had shewn,
The Douglas rent an earth-fast stone
From its deep bed, then heaved it high,
And sent the fragment through the sky,

A rood beyond the farthest mark ;
And still in Stirling's royal park,
The gray-haired sires, who know the past,
To strangers point the Douglas-cast,
And moralise on the decay
Of Scottish strength in modern day.

XXIV.

The vale with loud applauses rang,
The Ladies' Rock sent back the clang.
The King, with look unmoved, bestowed
A purse well filled with pieces broad.
Indignant smiled the Douglas proud,
And threw the gold among the crowd,
Who now, with anxious wonder, scan,
And sharper glance, the dark gray man ;
Till whispers rose among the throng,
That heart so free, and hand so strong,
Must to the Douglas blood belong ;
The old men marked and shook the head,
To see his hair with silver spread,
And winked aside, and told each son
Of feats upon the English done,
Ere Douglas of the stalwart hand
Was exiled from his native land.
The women praised his stately form,
Though wrecked by many a winter's storm ;
The youth with awe and wonder saw
His strength surpassing Nature's law.
Thus judged, as is their wont, the crowd,
Till murmurs rose to clamours loud.
But not a glance from that proud ring
Of peers who circled round the King,
With Douglas held communion kind,
Or called the banished man to mind ;
No, not from those who, at the chase,
Once held his side the honoured place,
Begirt his board, and, in the field,
Found safety underneath his shield :
For he, whom royal eyes disown,
When was his form to courtiers known !

XXV.

The Monarch saw the gambols flag,
And bade let loose a gallant stag,
Whose pride, the holiday to crown,
Two favourite greyhounds should pull down,
That venison free, and Bordeaux wine,
Might serve the archery to dine.
But Lufra—whom from Douglas' side
Nor bribe nor threat could e'er divide,
The fleetest hound in all the North—
Brave Lufra saw, and darted forth.
She left the royal hounds mid-way,
And dashing on the antlered prey,
Sunk her sharp muzzle in his flank,
And deep the flowing life-blood drank.
The King's stout huntsman saw the sport
By strange intruder broken short,
Came up, and, with his leash unbound,
In anger struck the noble hound.
—The Douglas had endured, that morn,
The King's cold look, the nobles' scorn,
And last, and worst to spirit proud,
Had borne the pity of the crowd ;
But Lufra had been fondly bred,
To share his board, to watch his bed,
And oft would Ellen, Lufra's neck,
In maiden glee, with garlands deck ;
They were such playmates, that with name
Of Lufra, Ellen's image came.
His stifled wrath is brimming high,
In darkened brow and flashing eye ;
As waves before the bark divide,
The crowd gave way before his stride ;
Needs but a buffet and no more,
The groom lies senseless in his gore.
Such blow no other hand could deal,
Though gauntleted in glove of steel.

XXVI.

Then clamoured loud the royal train,
And brandished swords and staves amain.

But stern the Baron's warning—'Back!
Back, on your lives, ye menial pack!
Beware the Douglas. Yes! behold,
King James! The Douglas, doomed of old,
And vainly sought for near and far,
A victim to atone the war,
A willing victim now attends,
Nor craves thy grace but for his friends.'
'Thus is my clemency repaid?
Presumptuous Lord!' the Monarch said;
'Of thy mis-proud ambitious clan,
Thou, James of Bothwell, wert the man,
The only man, in whom a foe
My woman-mercy would not know:
But shall a Monarch's presence brook
Injurious blow, and haughty look?—
What ho! the Captain of our Guard!
Give the offender fitting ward,—
Break off the sports!'—for tumult rose,
And yeomen 'gan to bend their bows—
'Break off the sports!' he said, and frowned,
'And bid our horsemen clear the ground.'

XXVII.

Then uproar wild and misarray
Marred the fair form of festal day.
The horsemen pricked among the crowd,
Repelled by threats and insult loud;
To earth are borne the old and weak,
The timorous fly, the women shriek;
With flint, with shaft, with staff, with bar,
The hardier urge tumultuous war.
At once round Douglas darkly sweep
The royal spears in circle deep,
And slowly scale the pathway steep,   .
While on the rear in thunder pour
The rabble with disordered roar.
With grief the noble Douglas saw
The Commons rise against the law,
And to the leading soldier said—
'Sir John of Hyndford! 'twas my blade
That knighthood on thy shoulder laid;

For that good deed, permit me then
A word with these misguided men.

XXVIII.

'Here, gentle friends ! ere yet for me,
Ye break the bands of fealty.
My life, my honour, and my cause,
I tender free to Scotland's laws.
Are these so weak as must require
The aid of your misguided ire ?
Or, if I suffer causeless wrong,
Is then my selfish rage so strong,
My sense of public weal so low,
That, for mean vengeance on a foe,
Those cords of love I should unbind,
Which knit my country and my kind ?
Oh no ! Believe, in yonder tower
It will not soothe my captive hour,
To know those spears our foes should dread,
For me in kindred gore are red ;
To know, in fruitless brawl begun,
For me, that mother wails her son ;
For me, that widow's mate expires ;
For me, that orphans weep their sires ;
That patriots mourn insulted laws,
And curse the Douglas for the cause.
O let your patience ward such ill,
And keep your right to love me still !'

XXIX.

The crowd's wild fury sunk again
In tears, as tempests melt in rain.
With lifted hands and eyes, they prayed
For blessings on his generous head,
Who for his country felt alone,
And prized her blood beyond his own.
Old men, upon the verge of life,
Blessed him who stayed the civil strife ;
And mothers held their babes on high,
The self-devoted Chief to spy,
Triumphant over wrongs and ire,
To whom the prattlers owed a sire ;

Even the rough soldier's heart was moved;
As if behind some bier beloved,
With trailing arms and drooping head,
The Douglas up the hill he led,
And at the Castle's battled verge,
With sighs resigned his honoured charge.

XXX.

The offended Monarch rode apart,
With bitter thought and swelling heart,
And would not now vouchsafe again
Through Stirling streets to lead his train.
'O Lennox, who would wish to rule
'This changeling crowd, this common fool?
Hear'st thou,' he said, 'the loud acclaim
With which they shout the Douglas name?
With like acclaim the vulgar throat
Strained for King James their morning note;
With like acclaim they hailed the day,
When first I broke the Douglas' sway;
And like acclaim would Douglas greet,
If he could hurl me from my seat.
Who o'er the herd would wish to reign,
Fantastic, fickle, fierce, and vain!
Vain as the leaf upon the stream,
And fickle as a changeful dream;
Fantastic as a woman's mood,
And fierce as Frenzy's fevered blood.
Thou many-headed monster-thing,
O who would wish to be thy King!—

XXXI.

'But soft! what messenger of speed
Spurs hitherward his panting steed?
I guess his cognizance afar—
What from our cousin, John of Mar?'—
'He prays, my liege, your sports keep bound
Within the safe and guarded ground:
For some foul purpose yet unknown—
Most sure for evil to the throne—
The outlawed Chieftain, Roderick Dhu,
Has summoned his rebellious crew;

'Tis said, in James of Bothwell's aid
These loose banditti stand arrayed.
The Earl of Mar, this morn, from Doune,
To break their muster marched, and soon
Your grace will hear of battle fought ;
But earnestly the Earl besought,
Till from such danger he provide,
With scanty train you will not ride.'

XXXII.

' Thou warn'st me I have done amiss—
I should have earlier looked to this :
I lost it in this bustling day.
—Retrace with speed thy former way,
Spare not for spoiling of thy steed,
The best of mine shall be thy meed.
Say to our faithful Lord of Mar,
We do forbid the intended war :
Roderick, this morn, in single fight,
Was made our prisoner by a knight ;
And Douglas hath himself and cause
Submitted to our kingdom's laws.
The tidings of their leaders lost
Will soon dissolve the mountain host,
Nor would we that the vulgar feel,
For their Chief's crimes, avenging steel.
Bear Mar our message, Braco ; fly !'—
He turned his steed—' My liege, I hie—
Yet, ere I cross this lily lawn,
I fear the broadswords will be drawn.'
The turf the flying courser spurned,
And to his towers the King returned.

XXXIII.

Ill with King James's mood that day,
Suited gay feast and minstrel lay ;
Soon were dismissed the courtly throng,
And soon cut short the festal song.
Nor less upon the saddened town
The evening sunk in sorrow down.
The burghers spoke of civil jar,
Of rumoured feuds and mountain war,

Of Moray, Mar, and Roderick Dhu,
All up in arms—the Douglas too,
They mourned him pent within the hold
'Where stout Earl William was of old.'
And there his word the speaker staid,
And finger on his lip he laid,
Or pointed to his dagger blade.
But jaded horsemen, from the west,
At evening to the Castle pressed ;
And busy talkers said they bore
Tidings of fight on Katrine's shore ;
At noon the deadly fray begun,
And lasted till the set of sun.
Thus giddy rumour shook the town,

NOTES

AFTER a hasty morning meal the two start upon their journey, and the Gael's enquiries as to the knight's object in thus venturing in these wilds without a pass from the chief lead to an interesting conversation betwixt them. Fitz-James shows that Roderick's suspicions of a war-gathering are mistaken, but hints that his preparations may possibly lead to an encounter which had not been intended. He avows his enmity against Roderick, with whom he has vowed to match himself, and expresses the keenest desire to meet "the rebel chieftain and his band." "Have, then, thy wish," is the reply. His companion's shrill signal makes the whole hillside bristle with armed men, who have been lying *perdus* among the heather and the bracken, and the guide proclaims himself the very man whom he seeks. At a fresh sign the warriors disappear as suddenly as they sprang to light, and the two pursue their course. They pass the foot of Lake Vennachar, and at last reach the ford, which is the limit of Roderick's protection. There Fitz-James must defend himself with his own sword. The Gael, to make the fight more equal, throws away his targe, and thus the science which makes the good blade both sword and shield gives the knight the advantage over his adversary. The latter, thrice severely wounded, loses his sword, but makes a final effort, and springs at his opponent's throat. Clasped in his strong arms the knight falls under him, and the issue of the fight would have been changed had not Roderick turned giddy from loss of blood and missed his aim. Poor Blanche is thus revenged. The victor winds his bugle, and four attendants come galloping to the spot. Leaving two of them to look to the wounded man, he hastes with the others back to Stirling. As they come to the castle they catch sight of the Douglas, who comes to give himself up to the king in the hope of liberating the Græme, and of saving Roderick from a calamitous war. On his arrival he finds the town in a bustle of preparation for the burghers' sports, and determines to take part in them, and so introduce himself to the king. He proves victor in all that he undertakes, so that the multitude begin to suspect who he is; but the king gives him the prize as to an utter stranger. All this he bears patiently; but when his hound, Ellen's playfellow, is maltreated by the king's huntsman, he can bear it no longer, and with a sound cuff stretches the offender on the ground, and proclaims himself, and his purpose in coming. He is carried off captive to the castle. The people attempt a rescue, but are appeased by Douglas himself, and retire, though with gloomy forebodings of his fate.

While the king is brooding over the fickleness of the crowd, a messenger comes from the Earl of Mar to warn him that Clan-Alpine is rising, and that he must confine his sport to guarded ground. The earl himself is gone to quell the rising, and hopes soon to encounter the foe. James sends in all speed to stay the army's march, as Roderick is already a captive, and the people must not suffer for his crimes. But the message, as will be seen, comes too late.

This canto is by far the most powerful in the whole poem. It begins with one of those exquisite bits of description in which Scott excelled. The scene is not perhaps so lovely as Loch Katrine, but it is more varied. The conversation between the knight and his guide is skilfully directed, so as to shew us that Roderick, in his suspicions, has mistaken the king's purpose; that no raid was intended, but only a peaceful hunt. The ground of hostility between the Saxon and the Gael is carefully put forward, and the way well prepared for Roderick's declaring himself; and at the declaration we can hardly decide which most deserves our sympathy, the mountain chief, so often called barbarous and treacherous, who forbears to use his advantage, and respects the rights of hospitality; or the brave knight, who fronts this unexpected danger without flinching. The combat that shortly follows is related with much vigour, and we are kept in suspense as to the result to the last moment.

It is to be regretted that the rule of time, a canto to a day's action, should have given to the games that follow a place in the same canto. There is no real want of vigour in the description, but still it falls tamely after this. The only purpose that it serves is to make Douglas known, and to hint at the real cause of the unrest of the time; viz., the efforts of the Commons' King to curtail the power of the nobles.

Stanza 1.—This introductory stanza is well worked in with

the story. The morning beam "lights the fearful path on mountain side" which the two heroes of the poem are to traverse, and the comparison which it suggests enlists our sympathy for Roderick, who is to be the victim of defeat.

2.—*Dappled;* 'spotted,' 'variegated.' Akin to 'dab,' Icelandic 'depill,' a spot on a ground of different colour; 'deplottr,' dappled.—WEDGWOOD.

Muttered their soldier *matins by.* They were short and rude, as shown by the following couplet. 'By' seems to be inserted for the rhyme. It may mean 'near,' as "thou being *by*" (Milton); or, 'to mutter *by*' means 'to say quickly, so as to get them over.' Cp. stanza 20, "that is *by;*" *i.e.* 'over,' 'past.'

Bursting through. A piece of loose writing, for 'as they burst through.'

3.—*Flows, rose.* Another feeble sacrifice to rhyme.

Shingles. See note on iii. 7.

Heather black, that waved so high. Note how the details of this description are used in stanza 9—'shingles,' 'bracken,' 'broom.'

Dank. Probably the same word as 'damp.' Cp. Italian 'cambiare' and 'cangiare,' to change; English 'dimble' and 'dingle.' The meaning of the word is clearly seen in Milton's *Sonnet to Lawrence*—

"Now that the fields are *dank*, and ways are mire."

5.—Shows the mistake under which Roderick has been labouring, too late now for remedy.

Muster. Italian 'mostra,' Old French 'moustre,' 'a show,' 'review of troops.' From Latin 'monstro,' which is from 'moneo,' through 'monstrum,' 'a *warning* prodigy.' (The German 'muster,' which also means 'pattern,' 'sample,' shows the derivation more clearly.) Hence 'to *muster*' is 'to gather for review,' and so 'to gather' simply.

We were loth. The old construction is seen in the following:

"That other, be *him* loth or leef,
He may go pypen in an ivy leaf."—CHAUCER.

Regent. Albany. See next stanza. For the fact see canto ii. 12.

Ruffian. Italian 'ruffiano,' French 'rufien.' Appears to be connected with O.H.G. 'hruf,' 'scurf,' 'dirt;' English 'rough.' It is then applied in a moral sense. Dante has—

"Ruffian, baratti, e simile lordura."
"Ruffians and cheats, and such like filth."

6. —*His* due. Probably because *sovereignty* implies a *sovereign.*
> *While Albany, with feeble hand,*
> *Held borrowed truncheon of command.*

Albany was the son of a younger brother of James III., who
had been driven into exile by his brother's attempts on his life.
He was well received at the court of France, and his son was
made Lord High Admiral. To him the Scottish nobles turned
on the death of James IV., and invited him over to assume the
regency. He came in 1515, bringing with him a French retinue,
and French habits of rule, which soon made him unpopular in
Scotland. In the following year he returned to France on short
leave, and remained away till 1521. After a short stay in Scotland, he again went over to France for help against England,
and returned in September, 1523, with a considerable force; but,
owing to the distrust of the Scotch, he was obliged to abandon
his expedition. In 1524 he finally withdrew.

Mewed. French 'muer,' Latin 'mutare,' our 'moult.' Originally 'to cast the feathers,' 'to change them.' So the 'mew' or
'mews' was the place where hawks were confined while moult-
ing. The Royal *Mews* was the building where the king's hawks
were kept, which would be part of the stable offices, whence its
present meaning. To 'mew' is to 'pen' or 'shut up.' There
seems to be some inaccuracy in the history here. James V. was
only twelve years of age when Albany left, and Stirling was the
place he fled to for safety, when he threw off the yoke of Angus,
four years later.

Swain. Icelandic 'sveinn,' a boy, Danish 'svend,' a young
man, journeyman. A.S. 'swán,' a herdsman.

7. —*Steer.* A.S. 'styric,' German 'stier,' a young bull, ox, or
heifer.

Belong the target and claymore. These were the weapons of
the ancient Britons. Cp. Tacitus, *Agricola*, l. 36—
> "Ingentibus gladiis et brevibus cetris."

Pent. A.S. 'pyndan,' to confine; whence our 'pound,' '*pin-
fold.*' 'Pond' and 'pindar' are from the same root. The hilly
fastnesses are their natural fortress, in which they have been
cooped up by the aggressions of the Lowlanders.

Shock. A pile of sheaves, Dutch 'schokke,' German 'schock,'
possibly from the idea of a 'tuft,' 'branch.' Cp. 'shock' of
hair, Italian 'ciocco.' Akin to 'shake,' that which is shaken
together.

8. —*Meed.* German 'miethe,' Greek μισθος, reward.
Match me. Scott is rather fond of these reflexive forms. Cp.
> "Wilfred had *roused him* to reply."—*Rokeby*, ii. 13.

"*Stay thee*, fair, in Ravensheuch."—*Lay*, vi. 23.
"Enter and *rest thee* there a space."—*Lord of the Isles*, v. 21.
"*Mount thee* on the wightest steed."—*Lay*, i. 22.

9.—Compare with this the fears of Jarvis in *Rob Roy*, chap.
xxvii. : " Ill I winna say of him, for, forby that he 's my cousin,
we 're coming near his ain country, and there may be ane o' his
gillies ahint every whin-bush for what I ken." This incident,
like some other passages in the poem, illustrative of the character
of the ancient Gael, is not imaginary, but borrowed from fact.

Yawning hill. An instance of condensed epithet, as if the
hill had yawned and given, &c.

Beck. A nod or bow, A.S. 'beacen,' a sign, nod. Wedgwood quotes : " He (Hardicanute) made a law that every Inglis
man sal *bek*, and discover his hed quhen he met ane Dane."—
Bellenden.

10.—*Glint.* "To glance, gleam, or pass suddenly like a flash
of lightning."—JAMIESON. Danish 'glint,' a gleam, flash.
Cp. the slang "douse the *glim*," for 'put out the light.' Connected with 'glance,' 'glimpse,' 'glisten,' German 'glanz.'

Jack. The peasant's substitute for a coat of mail, known in
the time of the Commonwealth as a buff *jerkin*. It was a tunic
of leather, set with rings or bosses of iron. Meyrick says it
originated with the English, quoting a passage from the *Chro-
nicle of Bertrand du Guesclin* (time of Richard II.)—
　　　　　" Each had a *jack* above his hauberk."
It was buttoned down the front to the waist, and secured round
it by a girdle. (Fairholt, *Costume in England*). In the preparations for war with England (1454) every man worth twenty
marks is to have a *jack* with iron sleeves.—BURTON, ii. 431.
It was sometimes more effectually protected. In the *Monastery*,
chap. ix., Scott speaks of the *jack*, or doublet quilted with iron,
and, in the *Eve of St. John*, of the *plate-jack.*

11.—*Wont.* See i. 20. The word is used here in its original
sense as a participle.

12.—*Three mighty lakes.* Katrine, Achray, and Vennachar.
" The torrent which discharges itself from Loch Vennachar, the
lowest and eastmost of the three lakes which form the scenery
adjoining to the Trosachs, sweeps through a flat and extensive
moor called Bochastle. Upon a small eminence called the *Dun* of

Bochastle, and indeed on the plain itself, are some intrenchments, which have been thought Roman. There is, adjacent to Callender, a sweet villa, the residence of Captain Fairfoul, entitled the Roman Camp."—SCOTT.   This district is by many antiquaries held to be the scene of Agricola's final contest with the Scots in the *Mons Graupius.*   At Ardoch, near Dunblane, not far to the east of Menteith, is a very perfect Roman encampment, which is believed to have held his army. (The name *Grampians*, which has been given to the whole of this range of mountains, on the faith of Tacitus, appears from the MSS. to have arisen from a false reading.)

And his plaid.   So at Killiecrankie the Highlanders threw off their plaids and their brogues before beginning the fight.— MACAULAY, *History of England*, iii. 360.

13.—*Bred between the living and the dead.* See canto iii. 5.
Read.   'Interpreted,' A.S. 'rædan,' to advise, command, interpret; so the Scotch 'red,' 'rede.'   The connexion with 'ræd,' ready, plain, would suggest that it means *to make plain,* which will suit both meanings of the word.   For 'rede' = 'counsel' cp. *Hamlet,* i. 3—
 . "And recks not his own *rede.*"

14.—*Some vain carpet knight; i.e.* one who won his spurs, not on the battle-field by deeds of valour, but at court by dancing attendance on royalty.   A lord mayor knighted at a royal visit to the city is a carpet-knight.   Cp. *Twelfth Night,* iii. 4: "He is knight, dubbed with unhatched rapier, and on carpet consideration."
Ruth.   Pity.
Which thou wilt.   See stanza 11.
Scabbard.   The sheath or covering of a sword.   According to Wedgwood, a corruption of 'scaleboard,' thin board, of which it was made.   The word is used to denote this material.   "Some splints are made of *scabbard* and tin, sewed up in linen cloths."

15.—   *Ill fared it then with Roderick Dhu,*
    That on the field his targe he threw,
    For, trained abroad his arms to wield,
    Fitz-James's blade was sword and shield.
"A round target of light wood, covered with strong leather, and studded with brass or iron, was a necessary part of a Highlander's equipment.   In charging regular troops they received the thrust of the bayonet in this buckler, twisted it aside, and used the broad-sword against the encumbered soldier.   In the civil war of 1745, most of the front rank of the clans were thus armed; and Captain Grose informs us that in 1747, the privates

of the 42nd regiment, then in Flanders, were for the most part permitted to carry targets. The use of defensive armour, and particularly of the buckler, or target, was general in Queen Elizabeth's time, although that of the single rapier seems to have been occasionally practised much earlier. Rowland Yorke, however, who betrayed the fort of Zutphen to the Spaniards, for which good service he was afterwards poisoned by them, is said to have been the first who brought the rapier fight into general use."—SCOTT.

Cp. *Hamlet* iv. 7, 96. "And for your *rapier* most especially." Here and in Act v. sc. 2, Shakespeare implies that in his time Paris was the best fencing school.

Feint (Latin 'fingere,' French 'feindre'), to pretend to make a thrust, so as to distract the opponent's eye, and make him leave some part unguarded.

16.—*Recreant.* The Latin 'recredo' and its derivatives in the Romance languages, were used in the sense of 'surrender,' 'give up,' 'abate.' The participles, Italian 'ricredente,' French 'recréant,' were especially used of one who yields in battle, or in a judicial combat. To do so in the latter implied that a man's cause was not good enough for him to give his life for; so that '*recreant*' came to mean coward, convicted traitor.—WEDGWOOD.

Dagger. This completes the ordinary Highland equipment. He threw away his targe, his sword or claymore is forced from his hand, his dirk is left. Cp. Flora's Song in *Waverley*, chap. xxii.—

"The dirk and the target lie sordid with dust,
The bloodless claymore is but reddened with rust."

Triple steel. Cp. Horace, *Od.* i. 3, 9: "Illi robur et æs triplex circa pectus erat."

The odds. The chances of an event happening, or not happening, are either equal or unequal. For instance, if a coin is tossed head or tail must come up, and the chance of the one is as great as that of the other. In this case the chances are said to be *even*. If the chances are unequal, as, for instance, in throwing a die with six faces, where there is only one way for a given face to turn up, and five for it not to turn up, we might similarly say the chances are *odd*. But this would not tell us which event was most probable; so we say instead, *the odds* are *in favour* of the more likely event, *e.g.* of six not turning up; and *against* the less likely event, *e.g.* the six turning up; so *to turn the odds* is to transfer the chance of victory to him. As James's sword was sword and shield, and Roderick had thrown away his targe, he was fighting *against odds*.

Close; i.e. grapple; so we say to *close* with the enemy.

17.—Gallants. The A.S. 'gal,' German 'geil,' = 'light,' 'pleasant,' 'merry.' From it was formed the Italian and Spanish noun 'gala,' and from this a verb 'galare,' to keep *gala*, to pursue pleasure. Of this verb the Italian 'galante' is the participle (French 'galant,' our 'gallant'). Originally therefore it means one who knows how to make the most of pleasure-days; then one who knows how to please the fair sex (our 'gallánt'). Hence its meaning diverges. In English it means brave, in Italian honest, in French a man of pleasure.

Palfrey. An easy-going horse for riding, a lady's horse. French 'palefroi,' German 'pferd,' Mediæval Latin 'paraveredus, parafredus,' a hybrid word from Greek παρά, and 'veredus,' a post-horse; so an extra post-horse.

Boune. Ready. See iv. 8.

18.—Steel = 'spur.' Cf. i. 7, note.

Cross-bow. A bow placed athwart a stock. "It would send the 'quarell'—as the arrows were termed—a distance of forty rods." The cross-bowman had a *moulinet* and pulley for winding up his bow. "This operation is performed by fixing one foot in the sort of stirrup at the bottom [of the bow], and applying the wheels and lever to the string of the bow, and so winding it upward by the handle placed at its top."—FAIRHOLT.

Carhonie. About a mile from the mouth of Loch Vennachar.

Pricked; 'spurred,' 'rode quickly.' The word came to mean simply 'ride.' So Spenser, *Faerie Queen,* i. 1—

"A gentle knight was *pricking* on the plaine."

And in *Marmion,* v. 17—

"Northumbrian *prickers,* wild and rude."

Torry, Lendrick, Deanstown, Doune, Blair-Drummond, Ochtertyre, and *Kïer,* all lie on the banks of the Teith, between Callender and Stirling. Most of them are associated with personal friends of Sir W. Scott. *Craig-Forth* is between the two branches of the Forth, before and after the Teith joins it. During his visit to Cambusmore in 1809 Scott ascertained, by personal trial, that a good horseman might gallop from Loch Vennachar to Stirling in the time he has allotted to Fitz-James.

19.—Saint Serle. Lord Jeffrey remarks: "The king himself is in such distress for a rhyme as to be obliged to apply to one of the obscurest saints in the calendar." We have already noticed instances of this haste in the present canto.

The king must stand upon his guard. This seems a needless device to keep the secret: the courtiers of course know who Fitz-James is.

Postern. French 'posterne,' 'poterne,' from Low Latin 'posterula,' 'a back way.' The word is sometimes used for the gate itself.

20. — *Ye towers! within whose circuit dread*
    A Douglas by his sovereign bled.

In 1451 William, the then head of the house of Douglas, a man of great political activity at home and abroad, had, in order to secure his position, entered into a bond, or band, as it was called, with the Earls of Crawfurd and Ross.   On the 15th of January, 1452, James II. invited him to visit him at Stirling Castle, and after supper withdrew with him into an inner chamber.   After much talk upon public matters, the king bade him break these bands.   Douglas refused.   The king replied, 'Then this shall,' and stabbed him twice.   Sir Patrick Grey then came up, and finished the work with a pole-axe.—BURTON, ii. 425. In October, 1797, a human skeleton was found during some excavations in the garden, about eight yards from the window of the room where this happened.   As it was believed that the victim was buried on the spot, it is supposed that this was the skeleton of the Douglas.

Thou, O sad and fatal mound.   The "heading hill," north of the castle, used by James V. and his courtiers for sliding down on small sledges, from which it got the name of Hurley-Hacket. "Murdack Duke of Albany, Duncan Earl of Lennox, his father-in-law, and his two sons, Walter and Alexander Stuart, were executed at Stirling in 1425.   They were beheaded upon an eminence without the castle walls, but making part of the same hill, from whence they could behold their strong castle of Doune and their extensive possessions."—SCOTT.

Franciscan steeple.   The Grey-friars' church was built by James IV. in 1494, on the slope of the Castle Rock.   James VI. was crowned here in July, 1567.

Pageant.   Possibly from Latin 'compaginata,' 'fitted together.' Originally the scaffolding or movable platform on which mystery plays were acted.   It is called 'pagina' in old documents.   Then it was transferred to that which was exhibited, whether it were a dumb show or a dramatic performance.   In the *Chester Mysteries* each drama is introduced in the form, "Incipit *pagina* prima de celi, &c., creacione."

Morrice-dancers.   Originally 'Moriscos,' or '*Moorish* dancers.' The dance was probably the Spanish 'fandango;' but it was in England soon combined with the national May-day pageant of Robin Hood and Maid Marian, the Queen of the May.   It required five characters, though the number was sometimes extended.   They were Robin Hood, Maid Marian, a friar (Robin Hood's chaplain, Friar Tuck), a minstrel, and a clown. The hobby-horse was generally added to them, and often the usher of the bower, or gentleman usher.   Most of these characters are found in Ben Jonson's *Sad Shepherd*, already referred to, which is a thoroughly poetical version of this pageant.   One

distinctive feature of the morris-dancer, and indicative of his
origin, was the wearing bells upon the heel. (See stanza 22, and
note.) The dance was kept up till the earlier part of the present
century. Hone saw it in London in 1826. In Oxfordshire it is
said to be still ·practised, though a few ribbons are the only remains of the old costume. (CHAMBERS, *Book of Days*, i. 630-
633.) There is a description of the play in the *Abbot*, ch. xiv.,
and Scott's note. Its popularity was a great stumbling-block to
the Reformers on each side of the Border. It was forbidden in
Scotland by statute in 1555, but "it would seem, from the com-
plaints of the General Assembly of the Kirk, that these profane
festivities were continued down to 1592. Bold Robin was, to
say the least, equally successful in maintaining his ground against
the reformed clergy of England ; for the simple and evangelical
Latimer complains of coming to a country church, where the
people refused to hear him because it was Robin Hood's day ;
and his mitre and rochet were fain to give way to the village
pastime."—SCOTT.

Play my prize. Cp. *Odyssey*, xxiv. 89 : ζώννυνται τε νέοι καὶ
ἐπεντύνονται ἄεθλα : "get ready for the prizes," meaning the
contest.

21.—*The Castle gates were open flung.* Stirling Castle was
already one of the principal fortresses of Scotland in the twelfth
century, and about the beginning of the fifteenth became a royal
residence. A palace was erected within its walls by James V.,
with whose history, as we have seen, it is intimately associated.
It stands upon a lofty rock, which commands the Forth. The
slope which connects it with the plain is occupied by the town
of Stirling.

Jennet. A small Spanish horse ; from Spanish 'ginete,' a
light horse soldier ; said to come from the Arabic 'diund,' a
soldier. (Connected by others with the Greek γύμνητες.) From
the soldier it was transferred, in French and English, to the
horse which he rode.

Long live the Commons' King, King James! The lines that
follow explain the policy which in great part led to this name.
James had done what was done by Henry VII. in England,
and by Louis XI. in France ; that is, had striven to check the
lawless power of the nobles, and had sought the alliance of the
commons, or people of the towns. Shortly after the fall of
Angus, the Earl of Argyle was deprived of the lieutenancy of
the Isles, a step which led some of the Lowland lords to transfer
their allegiance to England. Later (1540), when the king made
a progress in the north, he took possession of some of the Highland chiefs, and brought them southward in captivity, as sureties
for the good behaviour of their clans. (BURTON, iii. 175.)

22.—*The Castle-park* lies to the south of the Castle, from which it is separated by the king's garden and the esplanade, which parts the Castle from the town.

Chequered.   In allusion to the gay dresses of the *pageants*, or of the morris-dancers, whose dress is described as of white fustian spangled.

Morricers, with bell at heel.   The bell at heel was indispensable, but this was not necessarily all.   In a description of a morris-dancer's dress, given in a note (*s*) to the *Fair Maid of Perth*, we find that it has 252 small bells in sets of twelve at regular musical intervals ; so that, like the old woman of Banbury, music would go with him wherever he went.

Butts.   French ' buttes,' literally the mound of earth which supports the target.   (Same root as ' boss,' iv. 5.)

Cowl.   Latin ' cucullus,' a hood attached to the long tunic, so as to be pulled over the head ; hence the proverb, '' Cucullus non facit monachum.''

Scathelocke and *Scarlet* are two of the characters in Ben Jonson's play.   Will Scarlet is mentioned in the ballad of *Robin Hood's Death*, in Percy's MS. ; Friar Tuck, the clerk of Copmanhurst, in *Ivanhoe*.   The games that follow remind us of the funeral games for Patroclus in the *Iliad*, and for Anchises in the *Æneid*, though they are treated with distinct originality.   The stag-hunt is Scott's own.

Stake ; i.e. prize.

Wight.   Creature ; *i.e.* commonest archer.   A.S. 'wiht,' from which we have also ' whit.'   Cp. German ' bösewicht,' a good-for-nothing fellow.   It was once used of fairies, spirits ; so Chaucer, *Miller's Tale*—

'' I crouche thee from elves and from *wights*.''

Part of this scene is taken from a story, reported by Hume of Godscroft, which has been worked up into a ballad by Mr. Finlay (*Scottish Historical and Romantic Ballads*.   Glasgow, 1808).   It is introduced as follows—

'' Our nobles they hae sworn an aith?
   An they gart our young king swear the same,
   That as lang as the crown was on his head
   He wad speak to nane o' the Douglas name.

'' An wasna this a wearifou aith ;
   For the crown frae his head had been tint and gane,
   Gin the Douglas hand hadna held it on,
   Whan anither to help him there was nane.

'' An the king frae that day grew dowie and wae ;
   For he liked in his heart the Douglas weel ;
   For his foster-brither was Jamie o' Parkhead,
   An Archie o' Kilspindie was his *Grey Steill*.

" But Jamie was banisht, an' Archy baith,
     An' they lived lang, lang ayont the sea,
Till a' had forgotten them but the king,
     An' he whiles said wi' a watery e'e,
Gin they think on me as I think on them,
     I wot their life is but drearie."

The king goes out hunting with his nobles, and is returning to
" Snawdon Tower,"

" When Murray cried loud—Wha's yon I see?
     Like a Douglas he looks, baith dark and grim,
And for a' his sad and weary pace,
     Like them he's richt stark o' arm and limb.

The king's heart lap, and he shouted wi' glee:
     Yon stalwarth makedom I ken richt weel,
And I'se wad in pawn the hawk on my han',
     It's Archie Kilspindie, my ain Gray Steill;
We maun gie him grace o' a' his race;
     For Kilspindie was trusty, ay and leal."

But his nobles, some sadly, some sternly, remind him of his
oath, and with heart "yearnin and like to brast," he spoke
haughtily to his old friend, who would not be thrown off, but
kept up with the cavalcade to the castle gate. The king looked
back right wistfully, but left him there. The poor man begged
for a draught of cold water; but no one durst give it him, so
strict was the ban. The king, when he heard of it, was "red-
wood furious," and—

" A' fu' sad at the table he sat him down,
     An he spak but ae word at the dine:
O I wish my warst fae were but a king
     Wi' as cruel counsellours as mine!"

23.—*For life is Hugh of Larbert lame.* Lord Jeffrey objects
to this expression as intolerable. It seems to me to have the
great merit of setting the whole struggle before us in a line,
without wasting any words of description upon it. *Larbert* is in
Stirlingshire, about ten miles south of Stirling. In its church
Bruce, the Abyssinian traveller, is buried.
     Alloa. On the other side of the Forth, in Clackmannan.
     A golden ring. The ordinary prize for wrestling was a ram
and a ring. Cp. Chaucer, *Coke's Tale of Gamelyn*, 169—

" Litheth, and lestneth, and holdeth your tonge,
     And ye schul heere talkyng of Gamelyn the yonge.
Ther was ther bysiden cry'ed a wrastling,
     And therfor ther was sette up a ram and a ryng."

And moralise on the decay
Of Scottish strength in modern day.
So in Homer and Virgil, the great victors are generally those of
a former generation, who astonish the younger men by exploits
to which they can never attain. (Hom. *Il.* v. 303, xii. 447;
Virg. *Æn.* xii. 899.) Cp. with this stanza the putting the bar
in Homer, *Il.* xxiii.

24.—*Ladies' Rock.* A hillock in the "valley," from which
the ladies of the court witnessed the tourney.
Douglas of the stalwart hand. See note on canto iv. 27.
For an illustration of the close of this stanza compare the
scene of Wolsey's downfall, *Henry VIII.* act iii. scene 2.

25.—*Gambols.* O.E. 'gambauld,' French 'gambade,' literally skipping, dancing, from 'gambe,' an old form of 'jambe,'
a leg; and that from Celtic root 'cam,' crooked ("This is clean
cam."—SHAKESPEARE, *Coriolanus*). Cp. 'camera,' an arch;
Greek καμπή, a bending.
Buffet. A blow, slap, from 'buff,' an imitation of the sound.
Cp. French 'soufflet,' a slap in the face, from 'souffler,' to
blow.

26.—*Pack.* Rabble. See i. 4, and note.

27.—*Hyndford.* A village on the Clyde, three or four miles
south-east of Lanark.

28.—*Fealty.* French 'féelté,' Latin 'fidelitas,' 'faith,' 'loyalty.'
Widow's mate expires. A bold instance of prolepsis. She is
not a widow till he expires.

29.—*As tempests melt in rain.* This comparison is a common
one. Cp. Tennyson, song in the *Princess*—
　　　　"Like summer tempest came her tears."
Shakespeare, *Venus and Adonis*, l. 965—
　　"But, like a stormy day, now wind, now rain,
　　　Sighs dry her cheeks, tears make them wet again."
Verge. French 'verge,' Latin 'virga,' 'the wand borne by
the officer of a court.' Within the *verge* of the court = within
the limits of his authority; and hence 'verge'='limit,' 'edge.'

30.—*Thou many-headed monster-thing.* Cp. *Coriolanus*, i. 1—
　　　　　　"He that depends
　　Upon your favour swims with fins of lead,
　　And hews down oaks with rushes.
　　With every minute do you change your mind,

And call him noble that was now your hate,
Him vile that was your garland."
2 *King Henry IV.* i. 3—
"An habitation giddy and unsure
Hath he that buildeth on the vulgar heart."

31.—*Cognizance.* French 'connaissance,' 'knowledge.' A
knight in full armour, with his vizor down, so that his face was
hid, was recognized by his crest or heraldic coat; here the sable
pale.

II.

At dawn the towers of Stirling rang
With soldier-step and weapon-clang,
While drums, with rolling note, foretell
Relief to weary sentinel.
Through narrow loop and casement barred
The sunbeams sought the Court of Guard,
And, struggling with the smoky air,
Deadened the torches' yellow glare.
In comfortless alliance shone
The lights through arch of blackened stone,
And shewed wild shapes in garb of war,
Faces deformed with beard and scar,
All haggard from the midnight watch,
And fevered with the stern debauch ;
For the oak table's massive board,
Flooded with wine, with fragments stored,
And beakers drained, and cups o'erthrown,
Shewed in what sport the night had flown.
Some, weary, snored on floor and bench ;
Some laboured still their thirst to quench ;
Some, chilled with watching, spread their hands
O'er the huge chimney's dying brands,
While round them, or beside them flung,
At every step their harness rung.

III.

These drew not for their fields the sword,
Like tenants of a feudal lord,
Nor owned the patriarchal claim
Of Chieftain in their leader's name ;
Adventurers they, from far who roved,
To live by battle, which they loved.
There the Italian's clouded face,
The swarthy Spaniard's there you trace ;
The mountain-loving Switzer there
More freely breathed in mountain-air ;
The Fleming there despised the soil,
That paid so ill the labourer's toil ;
Their rolls shewed French and German name ;
And merry England's exiles came,

To share, with ill-concealed disdain,
Of Scotland's pay the scanty gain.
All brave in arms, well trained to wield
The heavy halberd, brand, and shield ;
In camps licentious, wild, and bold ;
In pillage fierce and uncontrolled ;
And now, by holytide and feast,
From rules of discipline released.

IV.

They held debate of bloody fray,
Fought 'twixt Loch Katrine and Achray.
Fierce was their speech, and, 'mid their words,
Their hands oft grappled to their swords ;
Nor sunk their tone to spare the ear
Of wounded comrades groaning near,
Whose mangled limbs, and bodies gored,
Bore token of the mountain sword,
Though, neighbouring to the Court of Guard,
Their prayers and feverish wails were heard ;
Sad burden to the ruffian joke,
And savage oath by fury spoke !—
At length up-started John of Brent,
A yeoman from the banks of Trent ;
A stranger to respect or fear,
In peace a chaser of the deer,
In host a hardy mutineer,
But still the boldest of the crew,
When deed of danger was to do.
He grieved, that day, their games cut short,
And marred the dicer's brawling sport,
And shouted loud, ' Renew the bowl !
And, while a merry catch I troll,
Let each the buxom chorus bear,
Like brethren of the brand and spear.'

V.

SOLDIER'S SONG.

Our vicar still preaches that Peter and Poule
Laid a swinging long curse on the bonny brown bowl,

That there's wrath and despair in the jolly black-jack,
And the seven deadly sins in a flagon of sack ;
Yet whoop, Barnaby! off with thy liquor,
Drink upsees out, and a fig for the vicar !

Our vicar he calls it damnation to sip
The ripe ruddy dew of a woman's dear lip,
Says, that Beelzebub lurks in her kerchief so sly,
And Apollyon shoots darts from her merry black eye ;
Yet whoop, Jack! kiss Gillian the quicker,
Till she bloom like a rose, and a fig for the vicar !

Our vicar thus preaches—and why should he not?
For the dues of his cure are the placket and pot ;
And 'tis right of his office poor laymen to lurch,
Who infringe the domains of our good Mother Church.
Yet whoop, bully-boys ! off with your liquor,
Sweet Marjorie's the word, and a fig for the vicar !

VI.

The warder's challenge, heard without,
Staid in mid-roar the merry shout.
A soldier to the portal went—
' Here is old Bertram, sirs, of Ghent ;
And—beat for jubilee the drum !
A maid and minstrel with him come.'
Bertram, a Fleming, gray and scarred,
Was entering now the Court of Guard.
A harper with him, and in plaid
All muffled close, a mountain maid,
Who backward shrunk to 'scape the view
Of the loose scene and boisterous crew.
' What news ?' they roared :—' I only know,
From noon till eve we fought with foe,
As wild and as untameable
As the rude mountains where they dwell ;
On both sides store of blood is lost,
Nor much success can either boast.'—
' But whence thy captives, friend ? Such spoil
As theirs must needs reward thy toil.
Old dost thou wax, and wars grow sharp :
Thou now hast glee-maiden and harp !

: Get thee an ape, and trudge the land,
The leader of a juggler band.'

VII.

' No, comrade ; no such fortune mine.
After the fight these sought our line,
That aged harper and the girl,
And, having audience of the Earl,
Mar bade I should purvey them steed,
And bring them hitherward with speed.
Forbear your mirth and rude alarm,
For none shall do them shame or harm.'
' Hear ye his boast ? ' cried John of Brent,
Ever to strife and jangling bent ;
' Shall he strike doe beside our lodge,
And yet the jealous niggard grudge
To pay the forester his fee ?
I 'll have my share, howe'er it be,
Despite of Moray, Mar, or thee.'
Bertram his forward step withstood ;
And, burning in his vengeful mood,
Old Allan, though unfit for strife,
Laid hand upon his dagger-knife ;
But Ellen boldly stepped between,
And dropped at once the tartan screen:
So, from his morning cloud, appears
The sun of May, through summer tears.
The savage soldiery, amazed,
As on descended angel gazed ;
Even hardy Brent, abashed and tamed,
Stood half admiring, half ashamed.

VIII.

Boldly she spoke—' Soldiers, attend ;
My father was the soldier's friend ;
Cheered him in camps, in marches led,
And with him in the battle bled.
Not from the valiant, or the strong,
Should exile's daughter suffer wrong.'
Answered De Brent, most forward still
In every feat or good or ill—

'I shame me of the part I played:
And thou an outlaw's child, poor maid!
An outlaw I by, forest laws,
And merry Needwood knows the cause.
Poor Rose—if Rose be living now,'
He wiped his iron eye and brow,
'Must bear such age, I think. as thou.
Hear ye, my mates;—I go to call
The Captain of our watch to hall:
There lies my halbert on the floor;
And he that steps my halbert o'er,
To do the maid injurious part,
My shaft shall quiver in his heart!—
Beware loose speech, or jesting rough:
Ye all know John de Brent.   Enough.'

IX.

Their Captain came, a gallant young—
(Of Tullibardine's house he sprung).
Nor wore he yet the spurs of knight;
Gay was his mien, his humour light,
And, though by courtesy controlled,
Forward his speech, his bearing bold.
The high-born maiden ill could brook
The scanning of his curious look
And dauntless eye;—and yet, in sooth,
Young Lewis was a generous youth;
But Ellen's lovely face and mien,
Ill suited to the garb and scene,
Might lightly bear construction strange,
And give loose fancy scope to range.
Welcome to Stirling towers, fair maid!
Come ye to seek a champion's aid,
On palfrey white, with harper hoar,
Like errant damosel of yore?
Does thy high quest a knight require,
Or may the venture suit a squire?'—
Her dark eye flashed;—she paused and sighed—
'O what have I to do with pride!—
—Through scenes of sorrow, shame, and strife,
A suppliant for a father's life,

I crave an audience of the King.
Behold, to back my suit, a ring,
The royal pledge of grateful claims,
Given by the Monarch to Fitz-James.'

X.

The signet-ring young Lewis took,
With deep respect and altered look;
And said—'This ring our duties own;
And pardon, if to worth unknown,
In semblance mean obscurely veiled,
Lady, in aught my folly failed.
Soon as the day flings wide his gates,
The King shall know what suitor waits.
Please you, meanwhile, in fitting bower
Repose you till his waking hour;
Female attendance shall obey
Your hest, for service or array.
Permit I marshal you the way.'
But, ere she followed, with the grace
And open bounty of her race,
She bade her slender purse be shared
Among the soldiers of the guard.
The rest with thanks their guerdon took;
But Brent, with shy and awkward look,
On the reluctant maiden's hold
Forced bluntly back the proffered gold;
⊦' Forgive a haughty English heart,
And O forget its ruder part!
The vacant purse shall be my share,
Which in my barret-cap I'll bear
Perchance in jeopardy of war,
Where gayer crests may keep afar.'
With thanks—'twas all she could—the maid
His rugged courtesy repaid. ✛

XI.

When Ellen forth with Lewis went,
Allan made suit to John of Brent:—
'My lady safe, O let your grace
Give me to see my master's face!

His minstrel I—to share his doom
Bound from the cradle to the tomb.
Tenth in descent, since first my sires
Waked for his noble house their lyres,
Nor one of all the race was known
But prized its weal above their own.
With the Chief's birth begins our care ;
Our harp must soothe the infant heir,
Teach the youth tales of fight, and grace
His earliest feat of field or chase ;
In peace, in war, our rank we keep,
We cheer his board, we soothe his sleep,
Nor leave him till we pour our verse—
A doleful tribute !—o'er his hearse.
Then let me share his captive lot ;
It is my right—deny it not !'—
' Little we reck,' said John of Brent,
' We southern men, of long descent ;
Nor wot we how a name—a word—
Makes clansmen vassals to a lord :
Yet kind my noble landlord's part.—
God bless the house of Beaudesert !
And, but I loved to drive the deer,
More than to guide the labouring steer,
I had not dwelt an outcast here.
Come, good old Minstrel, follow me ;
Thy Lord and Chieftain shalt thou see.'

XII.

Then, from a rusted iron hook,
A bunch of ponderous keys he took,
Lighted a torch, and Allan led
Through grated arch and passage dread.
Portals they passed, where, deep within,
Spoke prisoner's moan, and fetters' din ;
Through rugged vaults, where, loosely stored,
Lay wheel, and axe, and headsman's sword,
And many an hideous engine grim,
For wrenching joint, and crushing limb,
By artist formed, who deemed it shame
And sin to give their work a name.

They halted at a low-browed porch,
And Brent to Allan gave the torch,
While bolt and chain he backward rolled,
And made the bar unhasp its hold.
They entered :—'twas a prison-room
Of stern security and gloom,
Yet not a dungeon ; for the day
Through lofty gratings found its way,
And rude and antique garniture
Decked the sad walls and oaken floor ;
Such as the rugged days of old
Deemed fit for captive noble's hold.
'Here,' said De Brent, 'thou mayst remain
Till the Leech visit him again.
Strict is his charge, the warders tell,
To tend the noble prisoner well.'
Retiring then the bolt he drew,
And the lock's murmurs growled anew.
Roused at the sound, from lowly bed
A captive feebly raised his head ;
The wondering Minstrel looked, and knew—
Not his dear Lord, but Roderick Dhu !
For, come from where Clan-Alpine fought,
They, erring, deemed the Chief he sought.

XIII.

As the tall ship, whose lofty prore
Shall never stem the billows more,
Deserted by her gallant band,
Amid the breakers lies astrand—
So, on his couch, lay Roderick Dhu !
And oft his fevered limbs he threw
In toss abrupt, as when her sides
Lie rocking in the advancing tides,
That shake her frame with ceaseless beat,
Yet cannot heave her from her seat ;—
O ! how unlike her course at sea !
Or his free step on hill and lea !—
Soon as the Minstrel he could scan,
—'What of thy lady ?—of my clan ?
My mother ?—Douglas ?—tell me all !
Have they been ruined in my fall ?

P

Ah, yes ! or wherefore art thou here !
Yet speak—speak boldly—do not fear.'—
(For Allan, who his mood well knew,
Was choked with grief and terror too.)—
'Who fought—who fled?—Old man, be brief ;—
Some might—for they had lost their Chief.
Who basely live?—who bravely died ?'—
'O, calm thee, Chief !' the Minstrel cried,
'Ellen is safe ;'—'For that thank Heaven !'
'And hopes are for the Douglas given ;—
The Lady Margaret too is well,
And, for thy clan—on field or fell,
Has never harp of minstrel told,
Of combat fought so true and bold.
Thy stately Pine is yet unbent,
Though many a goodly bough is rent.'

XIV.

The Chieftain reared his form on high,
And fever's fire was in his eye ;
But ghastly, pale, and livid streaks
Chequered his swarthy brow and cheeks.
—'Hark, Minstrel ! I have heard thee play,
With measure bold, on festal day,
In yon lone isle, . . . again where ne'er
Shall harper play, or warrior hear ! . . .
That stirring air that peals on high,
O'er Dermid's race our victory.—
Strike it !—and then (for well thou canst),
Free from thy minstrel-spirit glanced,
Fling me the picture of the fight,
When met my clan the Saxon might.
I 'll listen, till my fancy hears
The clang of swords, the crash of spears !
These grates, these walls, shall vanish then,
For the fair field of fighting men,   = *Alliteration*
And my free spirit burst away,
As if it soared from battle-fray.'
The trembling bard with awe obeyed—
Slow on the harp his hand he laid ;
But soon remembrance of the sight
He witnessed from the mountain's height,
With what old Bertram told at night,

Awakened the full power of song,
And bore him in career along ;—
As shallop launched on river's tide,
That slow and fearful leaves the side,
But, when it feels the middle stream,
Drives downward swift as lightning's beam.

XV.

BATTLE OF BEAL' AN DUINE.

'The minstrel came once more to view
The eastern ridge of Benvenue,
For, ere he parted, he would say
Farewell to lovely Loch Achray—
Where shall he find, in foreign land,
So lone a lake, so sweet a strand !
There is no breeze upon the fern,
    No ripple on the lake,
Upon her eyry nods the erne,
    The deer has sought the brake ;
The small birds will not sing aloud,
    The springing trout lies still,
So darkly glooms yon thunder-cloud,
That swathes, as with a purple shroud,
    Benledi's distant hill.
Is it the thunder's solemn sound
    That mutters deep and dread,
Or echoes from the groaning ground
    The warrior's measured tread ?
Is it the lightning's quivering glance
    That on the thicket streams,
Or do they flash on spear and lance
    The sun's retiring beams ?
—I see the dagger-crest of Mar,
I see the Moray's silver star,
Wave o'er the cloud of Saxon war,
That up the lake comes winding far !
To hero bound for battle-strife,
    Or bard of martial lay,
'Twere worth ten years of peaceful life,
    One glance at their array !

XVI.

'Their light-armed archers far and near
  Surveyed the tangled ground,
Their centre ranks, with pike and spear,
  A twilight forest frowned,
Their barbed horsemen, in the rear,
  The stern battalia crowned.
No cymbal clashed, no clarion rang,
  Still were the pipe and drum;
Save heavy tread, and armour's clang,
  The sullen march was dumb.
There breathed no wind their crests to shake,
  Or wave their flags abroad;
Scarce the frail aspen seemed to quake,
  That shadowed o'er their road.
Their vanward scouts no tidings bring,
  Can rouse no lurking foe,
Nor spy a trace of living thing,
  Save when they stirred the roe;
The host moves, like a deep-sea wave,
Where rise no rocks its pride to brave,
  High-swelling, dark, and slow.
The lake is passed, and now they gain
A narrow and a broken plain,
Before the Trosachs' rugged jaws;
And here the horse and spearmen pause,
While, to explore the dangerous glen,
Dive through the pass the archer-men.

XVII.

'At once there rose so wild a yell
Within that dark and narrow dell,
As all the fiends, from heaven that fell,
Had pealed the banner-cry of hell!
  Forth from the pass in tumult driven,
  Like chaff before the wind of heaven,
    The archery appear:
  For life! for life! their plight they ply—
  And shriek, and shout, and battle-cry,
  And plaids and bonnets waving high,
  And broadswords flashing to the sky,
    Are maddening in the rear.

Onward they drive, in dreadful race,
 Pursuers and pursued;
Before that tide of flight and chase,
How shall it keep its rooted place,
 The spearmen's twilight wood?—
"Down, down," cried Mar, "your lances down!
 Bear back both friend and foe!"
Like reeds before the tempest's frown,
That serried grove of lances brown
 At once lay levelled low;
And closely shouldering side to side,
The bristling ranks the onset bide.
"We'll quell the savage mountaineer
 As their Tinchel cows the game!
They come as fleet as forest deer,
 We'll drive them back as tame."

XVIII.

'Bearing before them, in their course,
The relics of the archer force,
Like wave with crest of sparkling foam,
Right onward did Clan-Alpine come.
 Above the tide, each broadsword bright
 Was brandishing like beam of light,
 Each targe was dark below;
 And with the ocean's mighty swing,
 When heaving to the tempest's wing,
 They hurled them on the foe.
I heard the lance's shivering crash,
As when the whirlwind rends the ash;
I heard the broadsword's deadly clang,
As if an hundred anvils rang!
But Moray wheeled his rearward rank
Of horsemen on Clan-Alpine's flank,
 —"My banner-man, advance!
I see," he cried, "their column shake.—
Now, gallants! for your ladies' sake,
 Upon them with the lance!"—
The horsemen dashed among the rout,
 As deer break through the broom;
Their steeds are stout, their swords are out,
 They soon make lightsome room.

Clan-Alpine's best are backward borne—
 Where, where was Roderick then !
One blast upon his bugle-horn
 Were worth a thousand men.
And refluent through the pass of fear
 The battle's tide was poured ;
Vanished the Saxon's struggling spear,
 Vanished the mountain sword.
As Bracklinn's chasm, so black and steep,
 Receives her roaring linn,
As the dark caverns of the deep
 Suck the wild whirlpool in,
So did the deep and darksome pass
Devour the battle's mingled mass:
None linger now upon the plain,
Save those who ne'er shall fight again.

XIX.

Now westward rolls the battle's din,
That deep and doubling pass within.
—Minstrel, away ! the work of fate
Is bearing on : its issue wait,
Where the rude Trosachs' dread defile
Opens on Katrine's lake and isle.—
Gray Benvenue I soon repassed,
Loch Katrine lay beneath me cast.
 The sun is set ;—the clouds are met,
 The lowering scowl of heaven
 An inky hue of livid blue
 To the deep lake has given ;
Strange gusts of wind from mountain glen
Swept o'er the lake, then sunk agen.
I heeded not the eddying surge,
Mine eye but saw the Trosachs' gorge,
Mine ear but heard the sullen sound,
Which like an earthquake shook the ground,
And spoke the stern and desperate strife
That parts not but with parting life,
Seeming, to minstrel-ear, to toll
The dirge of many a passing soul.
 Nearer it comes—the dim-wood glen
 The martial flood disgorged agen,

But not in mingled tide ;
The plaided warriors of the North
High on the mountain thunder forth
    And overhang its side ;
While by the lake below appears
The dark'ning cloud of Saxon spears.
At weary bay each shattered band,
Eyeing their foemen, sternly stand !
Their banners stream like tattered sail,
That flings its fragments to the gale,
And broken arms and disarray
Marked the fell havock of the day.

XX.

'Viewing the mountain's ridge askance,
The Saxon stood in sullen trance,
Till Moray pointed with his lance,
    And cried—" Behold yon isle !—
See ! none are left to guard its strand,
But women weak, that wring the hand :
'Tis there of yore the robber band
    Their booty wont to pile ;—
My purse, with bonnet-pieces store,
To him will swim a bow-shot o'er,
And loose a shallop from the shore.
Lightly we'll tame the war-wolf then,
Lords of his mate, and brood, and den."
Forth from the ranks a spearman sprung,
On earth his casque and corslet rung,
    He plunged him in the wave ;—
All saw the deed—the purpose knew,
And to their clamours Benvenue
    A mingled echo gave ;
The Saxons shout, their mate to cheer,
The helpless females scream for fear,
And yells for rage the mountaineer.
'Twas then, as by the outcry riven,
Poured down at once the lowering heaven ;
A whirlwind swept Loch Katrine's breast,
Her billows reared their snowy crest.
Well for the swimmer swelled they high,
To mar the Highland marksman's eye ;

For round him showered, 'mid rain and hail,
The vengeful arrows of the Gael.—
In vain.—He nears the isle—and lo!
His hand is on a shallop's bow.
—Just then a flash of lightning came,
It tinged the waves and strand with flame ;—
I marked Duncraggan's widowed dame,
Behind an oak I saw her stand,
A naked dirk gleamed in her hand :—
It darkened—but amid the moan
Of waves I heard a dying groan ;—
Another flash !—the spearman floats
A weltering corse beside the boats,
And the stern Matron o'er him stood,
Her hand and dagger streaming blood.

XXI.

'"Revenge ! revenge !" the Saxons cried,
The Gaels' exulting shout replied.
Despite the elemental rage,
Again they hurried to engage ;
But, ere they closed in desperate fight,
Bloody with spurring came a knight,
Sprung from his horse, and, from a crag,
Waved 'twixt the hosts a milk-white flag,
Clarion and trumpet by his side
Rung forth a truce-note high and wide,
While, in the Monarch's name, afar
A herald's voice forbade the war,
For Bothwell's lord, and Roderick bold,
Were both, he said, in captive hold.'
—But here the lay made sudden stand,
The harp escaped the Minstrel's hand !—
Oft had he stolen a glance, to spy
How Roderick brooked his minstrelsy:
At first, the Chieftain, to the chime,
With lifted hand, kept feeble time ;
That motion ceased—yet feeling strong
Varied his look as changed the song ;
At length, no more his deafened ear
The minstrel melody can hear ;

His face grows sharp—his hands are clenched,
As if some pang his heart-strings wrenched;
Set are his teeth, his fading eye
Is sternly fixed on vacancy;
Thus, motionless, and moanless, drew
His parting breath, stout Roderick Dhu!—
Old Allan-bane looked on aghast,
While grim and still his spirit passed;
But when he saw that life was fled,
He poured his wailing o'er the dead.

XXII.

LAMENT.

'And art thou cold and lowly laid,
Thy foemen's dread, thy people's aid,
Breadalbane's boast, Clan-Alpine's shade!
For thee shall none a requiem say?
—For thee—who loved the minstrel's lay,
For thee, of Bothwell's house the stay,
The shelter of her exiled line,
E'en in this prison-house of thine,
I'll wail for Alpine's honoured Pine!

'What groans shall yonder valleys fill!
What shrieks of grief shall rend yon hill!
What tears of burning rage shall thrill,
When mourns thy tribe thy battles done,
Thy fall before the race was won,
Thy sword ungirt ere set of sun!
There breathes not clansman of thy line,
But would have given his life for thine.—
O woe for Alpine's honoured Pine!

'Sad was thy lot on mortal stage!—
The captive thrush may brook the cage,
The prisoned eagle dies for rage.
Brave spirit, do not scorn my strain!
And, when its notes awake again,
Even she, so long beloved in vain,
Shall with my harp her voice combine,
And mix her woe and tears with mine,
To wail Clan-Alpine's honoured Pine.'

XXIII.

Ellen, the while, with bursting heart,
Remained in lordly bower apart,
Where played, with many-coloured gleams,
Through storied pane the rising beams.
In vain on gilded roof they fall,
And lightened up a tapestried wall,
And for her use a menial train
A rich collation spread in vain.
The banquet proud, the chamber gay,
Scarce drew the curious glance astray ;
Or, if she looked, 'twas but to say,
With better omen dawned the day
In that lone isle, where waved on high
The dun-deer's hide for canopy ;
Where oft her noble father shared
The simple meal her care prepared,
While Lufra, crouching by her side,
Her station claimed with jealous pride,
And Douglas, bent on woodland game,
Spoke of the chase to Malcolm Græme,
Whose answer, oft at random made,
The wandering of his thoughts betrayed.—
Those who such simple joys have known,
Are taught to prize them when they 're gone.
But sudden, see, she lifts her head !
The window seeks with cautious tread.
What distant music has the power
To win her in this woeful hour !
'Twas from a turret that o'erhung
Her latticed bower, the strain was sung.

XXIV.

LAY OF THE IMPRISONED HUNTSMAN.

' My hawk is tired of perch and hood,
My idle greyhound loathes his food,
My horse is weary of his stall,
And I am sick of captive thrall.
I wish I were as I have been,
Hunting the hart in forest green,

With bended bow and bloodhound free,
For that 's the life is meet for me.
I hate to learn the ebb of time,
From yon dull steeple's drowsy chime,
Or mark it as the sunbeams crawl,
Inch after inch, along the wall.
The lark was wont my matins ring,
The sable rook my vespers sing;
These towers, although a king's they be,
Have not a hall of joy for me.
No more at dawning morn I rise,
And sun myself in Ellen's eyes,
Drive the fleet deer the forest through,
And homeward wend with evening dew ;
A blithesome welcome blithely meet,
And lay my trophies at her feet,
While fled the eve on wing of glee—
That life is lost to love and me !'

XXV.

The heart-sick lay was hardly said,
The list'ner had not turned her head,
It trickled still, the starting tear,
When light a footstep struck her ear,
And Snowdoun's graceful Knight was near.
She turned the hastier, lest again
The prisoner should renew his strain.
' O welcome, brave Fitz-James,' she said ;
' How may an almost orphan maid
Pay the deep debt'——'O say not so !
To me no gratitude you owe.
Not mine, alas ! the boon to give,
And bid thy noble father live ;
I can be but thy guide, sweet maid,
With Scotland's King thy suit to aid.
No tyrant he, though ire and pride
May lay his better mood aside.
Come, Ellen, come !—'tis more than time,
He holds his court at morning prime.'
With beating heart, and bosom wrung,
As to a brother's arm she clung.

Gently he dried the falling tear,
And gently whispered hope and cheer;
Her faltering steps half led, half staid,
Through gallery fair and high arcade,
Till, at his touch, its wings of pride
A portal arch unfolded wide.

XXVI.

Within 'twas brilliant all and light,
A thronging scene of figures bright;
It glowed on Ellen's dazzled sight,
As when the setting sun has given
Ten thousand hues to summer even,
And from their tissue, fancy frames
Aërial knights and fairy dames.
Still by Fitz-James her footing staid;
A few faint steps she forward made,
Then slow her drooping head she raised,
And fearful round the presence gazed,
For him she sought, who owned this state,
The dreaded prince whose will was fate!—
She gazed on many a princely port,
Might well have ruled a royal court;
On many a splendid garb she gazed—
Then turned bewildered and amazed,
For all stood bare; and, in the room,
Fitz-James alone wore cap and plume.
To him each lady's look was lent;
On him each courtier's eye was bent;
Midst furs and silks and jewels sheen,
He stood, in simple Lincoln green,
The centre of the glittering ring—
And Snowdoun's Knight is Scotland's King.

XXVII.

As wreath of snow, on mountain-breast,
Slides from the rock that gave it rest,
Poor Ellen glided from her stay,
And at the Monarch's feet she lay;

No word her choking voice commands—
She shewed the ring—she clasped her hands.
O! not a moment could he brook,
The generous prince, that suppliant look!
Gently he raised her—and, the while,
Checked with a glance the circle's smile:
Graceful, but grave, her brow he kissed,
And bade her terrors be dismissed :—
'Yes, Fair; the wandering poor Fitz-James
The fealty of Scotland claims.
To him thy woes, thy wishes, bring;
He will redeem his signet ring.
Ask nought for Douglas;—yester even,
His prince and he have much forgiven:
Wrong hath he had from slanderous tongue,
I, from his rebel kinsmen, wrong.
We would not to the vulgar crowd
Yield what they craved with clamour loud;
Calmly we heard and judged his cause,
Our council aided, and our laws.
I stanched thy father's death-feud stern,
With stout De Vaux and gray Glencairn,
And Bothwell's Lord henceforth we own
The friend and bulwark of our Throne.—
But, lovely infidel, how now?
What clouds thy misbelieving brow?
Lord James of Douglas, lend thine aid;
Thou must confirm this doubting maid.'

XXVIII.

Then forth the noble Douglas sprung,
And on his neck his daughter hung.
The Monarch drank, that happy hour,
The sweetest, holiest draught of Power—
When it can say, with godlike voice,
Arise, sad Virtue, and rejoice!
Yet would not James the general eye
On Nature's raptures long should pry;
He stepped between—'Nay, Douglas, nay,
Steal not my proselyte away!
The riddle 'tis my right to read,
That brought this happy chance to speed.—

Yes, Ellen, when disguised I stray
In life's more low but happier way,
'Tis under name which veils my power,
Nor falsely veils—for Stirling's tower
Of yore the name of Snowdoun claims,
And Normans call me James Fitz-James.
Thus watch I o'er insulted laws,
Thus learn to right the injured cause.'—
Then, in a tone apart and low, ·
—'Ah, little trait'ress! none must know
What idle dream, what lighter thought,
What vanity full dearly bought,
Joined to thine eye's dark witchcraft, drew
My spell-bound steps to Benvenue,
In dangerous hour, and all but gave
Thy Monarch's life to mountain glaive!'
Aloud he spoke—'Thou still dost hold
That little talisman of gold,
Pledge of my faith, Fitz-James's ring—
What seeks fair Ellen of the King?'

XXIX.

Full well the conscious maiden guessed,
He probed the weakness of her breast;
But, with that consciousness, there came
A lightening of her fears for Græme,
And more she deemed the Monarch's ire
Kindled 'gainst him, who, for her sire,
Rebellious broadsword boldly drew;
And, to her generous feeling true,
She craved the grace of Roderick Dhu.—
'Forbear thy suit:—The King of kings
Alone can stay life's parting wings,
I know his heart, I know his hand,
Have shared his cheer, and proved his brand:—
My fairest earldom would I give
To bid Clan-Alpine's Chieftain live!—
Hast thou no other boon to crave?
No other captive friend to save?'
Blushing, she turned her from the King,
And to the Douglas gave the ring,

As if she wished her sire to speak
The suit that stained her glowing cheek.
'Nay, then, my pledge has lost its force,
And stubborn justice holds her course.
Malcolm, come forth!' And, at the word,
Down kneeled the Græme to Scotland's Lord.
'For thee, rash youth, no suppliant sues,
From thee may Vengeance claim her dues,
Who, nurtured underneath our smile,
Hast paid our care by treacherous wile,
And sought, amid thy faithful clan,
A refuge for an outlawed man,
Dishonouring thus thy loyal name.—
Fetters and warder for the Græme!'——
His chain of gold the King unstrung,
The links o'er Malcolm's neck he flung,
Then gently drew the glittering band,
And laid the clasp on Ellen's hand.

HARP of the North, farewell! The hills grow dark,
   On purple peaks a deeper shade descending;
In twilight copse the glow-worm lights her spark,
   The deer, half-seen, are to the covert wending.
Resume thy wizard elm! the fountain lending,
   And the wild breeze, thy wilder minstrelsy;
Thy numbers sweet with nature's vespers blending,
   With distant echo from the fold and lea,
And herd-boy's evening pipe, and hum of housing bee.

Yet, once again, farewell, thou Minstrel Harp!
   Yet, once again, forgive my feeble sway,
And little reck I of the censure sharp ·
   May idly cavil at an idle lay.
Much have I owed thy strains on life's long way,
   Through secret woes the world has never known,
When on the weary night dawned wearier day,
   And bitterer was the grief devoured alone.
That I o'erlive such woes, Enchantress! is thine own.

Hark! as my lingering footsteps slow retire,
  Some Spirit of the Air has waked thy string!
'Tis now a seraph bold, with touch of fire,
  'Tis now the brush of Fairy's frolic wing.
Receding now, the dying numbers ring
  Fainter and fainter down the rugged dell,
And now the mountain breezes scarcely bring
  A wandering witch-note of the distant spell—
And now, 'tis silent all!—Enchantress, fare thee well!

INTRODUCES us to the guard-room in Stirling Castle, amid the remains of the debauch which has followed the games of the previous day. While the few soldiers who remain awake are finishing their carouse, and talking over the rumours of yesterday's battle, they are joined by one of their mates, who has been in the field, and brings with him a maiden and a minstrel (Ellen and Allan Bane). They are at first disposed to treat the maiden roughly; but the sight of her innocent beauty, and her story of misfortune, touch the heart of one of the roughest in the company, who becomes her champion. Presently they are joined by the officer of the guard, who, at sight of Fitz-James's ring, commits the lady to proper care, while John of Brent, the guardsman who had interfered, grants Allan's request to see his master. But, fancying that the minstrel is one of Roderick's clansmen, he shows him into the wrong cell, where he finds the wounded chief. After anxious enquiries as to the safety of his kindred, Roderick asks news of the fight, and the minstrel, in spirited verse, sings the battle of Beal' an Duine, whose issue was left doubtful by the arrival of a messenger from the king with orders to stay the fight. But before he had finished his song the stern spirit had fled, and the minstrel's harp changes its tune from battle-song to death-dirge.

Meanwhile Ellen waits anxiously and impatiently for her audience with the king. At last Fitz-James appears to escort her to the audience chamber. Faltering, she looks round to find the king, and sees to her surprise that her companion alone remains covered, and "Snowdoun's knight is Scotland's king." He tells her how the feud with Douglas is at an end, and that her father is now to be "the friend and bulwark of his throne." But she has still the ring, still some boon to ask. She begs for Roderick's life, but that is past giving; and when she shrinks

Q

from further request, the king calls forth Malcolm, and throws over him a golden chain, which he gives to Ellen to keep.

Lord Jeffrey has objected to the guard-room scene and its accompanying song as the greatest blemish in the whole poem. The scene contrasts forcibly with the grace which characterises the rest ; but in a poem which rests its interest upon incident such a criticism seems overstrained.   It gives us a vigorous picture of a class of men who played a very important part in the history of the time, especially across the border ; men who, many of them outlaws, and fighting, not for country or for king, but for him who paid them best, were humoured with every license when they were not on strict military duty. The require-ments of the narrative might have been satisfied without these details, it is true ; but the use which Sir Walter has made of them—to show the power of beauty and innocence, and the chords of tenderness and goodness which lie ready to vibrate in the wildest natures—may surely reconcile us to such a piece of realism.

The scene of Roderick's death harmonizes well with his character. The minstrel's account of the battle the poet himself felt to be somewhat long, and yet it is difficult to see how it could be curtailed without spoiling it.   It is full of life and vigour, and our only cause of surprise is that the lay should only come to a *sudden* stand when it is really completed.

Stanza 1.—*Caitiff;* 'miserable wretch.' Latin 'captivus,' 'a captive;' whence Italian 'cattivo,' 'bad ;' French 'chétif.' Wiclif has, "He ledde caitifté *caitif;*" Chaucer, "The riche Crœsus, *caytif* in servage." Popular language has seized upon the degraded, despicable condition of the captive, and the mean-nesses which a servile position engenders, as in 'villain,' on the blunted morals of the serf; and in 'knave,' on the tricks and deceits of the serving-boy.

Kind nurse of men.   Shakespeare, 2 *Henry IV.* iii. 1—
          "O gentle sleep,
     Nature's soft nurse, how have I frighted thee?"

Pallet. According to Wedgwood, from the Gaelic 'peallaid,' 'a sheep-skin.' More probably the same as French 'paillasse,' 'a bed of straw.' French 'paille,' Latin 'palea.'

Gyve. A fetter; originally a log of wood attached to the ankle. Welsh 'gefyn,' Breton 'kef,' 'trunk of a tree;' French 'cep,' Latin 'cippus.''

Love-lorn. 'Lorn' is an old participle of 'leosen,' 'lesen,' our 'lose.' Cp. 'for-*lorn*,' German 'ver-*loren*.'

2.—*Beaker.* A drinking-vessel. Italian 'bicchiere,' German

'becher,' possibly from having a mouth or beak (Italian 'becco').
The same word as 'pitcher.' (DIEZ.)

Brands. Logs not wholly consumed ; partly *burnt*, but not
reduced to embers.

3.—*These drew not for their fields the sword,*
Like tenants of a feudal lord,
Nor owned the patriarchal claim
Of Chieftain in their leader's name ;
Adventurers they,   ●   ●

"The Scotch armies consisted chiefly of the nobility and barons,
with their vassals, who held lands under them, for military
service by themselves and tenants. The patriarchal influence
exercised by the heads of clans in the Highlands and Borders
was of a different nature, and sometimes at variance with feudal
principles. It flowed from the *Patria Potestas,* exercised by
the chieftain as representing the original father of the whole
name, and was often obeyed in contradiction to the feudal superior. James V. seems first to have introduced, in addition to
the militia furnished from these sources, the service of a small
number of mercenaries, who formed a body-guard, called the
Foot-Band."—SCOTT.

Clouded. Swarthy. The difference between the Italian and
Spanish complexion is very well indicated by these epithets.

Fleming. Some parts of the Netherlands, especially Flanders
and Brabant, were among the most fertile soil in Europe.
Motley (speaking of a time very shortly after this) says : "Thus
fifteen ages have passed away, and in the place of a horde of
savages, living among swamps and thickets, swarm three
millions of people, the most industrious, the most prosperous,
under the sun. Their cattle, grazing on the bottom of the sea,
are the finest in Europe, their agricultural products of more ex-
changeable value than if nature had made their land to overflow
with wine and oil."—*Dutch Republic, Introduction.*

Halberd. French 'hailebarde,' from the German 'helm,' a
handle, and 'barte,' an axe; so, an axe with a long handle.
The head generally consisted of a pointed spear-head with a
crescent-shaped blade attached to it axe-wise. It was introduced
into England in the reign of Edward IV., was the peculiar
weapon of the royal guard in Henry VII.'s time and after, and
continued in use till the time of George III. It was intended to
combine in one bill, glaive, and pike.

In camps licentious, wild, and bold. Like the French Scots-
guards, "They never mind what you do when you 're off duty ;
but miss you the roll-call, and see how they 'll arrange you."—
Old Mortality, ix. Cp. the picture of the soldiery in Schiller's
Wallenstein.

4.—*Debate.* Apparently little more than 'talk,' though from what follows it was somewhat quarrelsome.

Gored. Stained with blood; hence pierced so as to draw blood. The word is used now only of the wound made by the horn of an ox or some animal; but its use has not always been thus restricted; so "Pyrrhus—that *gored* the son before the father's face."—SURREY. (A.S. 'gor,' mud, mire; hence clotted blood.)

Burden. See ii. 18, note.

Yeoman. A countryman, from Gothic 'gavi,' German 'gau,' district, canton; so in Friesland 'gaeman' = 'villager.' The legal definition is 'he that hath free land of forty shillings by the year,' the ancient qualification for a voter in the election of knights of the shire.—BLACKSTONE.

Host; i.e. in war. The feudal vassal, when called upon to follow his lord to battle, was 'bannitus in hostem,' summoned by 'ban' against the enemy. The word 'hostis' came in this way to mean the *hostile expedition,* and so by an easy step the *army* on duty, and later any great gathering of men. In legal documents we find such expressions as "ne episcopi vexentur hostibus;" *i.e.* by demands of military service. "Hostem facere," to perform military service.

Buxom. Merry, blithe. A.S. 'buhsam,' from 'bugan,' to bow; German 'beugsam,' that bends easily; so Gower—

> "Unto him, which the head is,
> The membres *buxom* shall *bow.*"

Hence 'obedient,' 'pliable,' "*buxom* to the lawe."—*Piers Plowman.* The word became a special term of commendation to a young woman, as denoting flexibility and grace of figure, as well as gentle pliableness of disposition, and in the idea of liveliness and health gradually lost its original meaning. "A *buxom* landlady" now conveys far other ideas than that of a flexible figure. Cp. Gray, *Eton College*—

> "Theirs *buxom* health of rosy hue."

Milton uses it in both senses—

> "He with broad sails
> Winnowed the *buxom* air."

—*Par. Lost,* bk. ii. 842, following Spenser, *Faerie Queene,* i. 9, 37.

> "A daughter fair,
> So *buxom,* blithe, and debonnair."—*L'Allegro,* 24.

Scott uses it in *Marmion,* iii. 4 in its original sense—

> "Such *buxom* chief shall lead his host
> From India's fires to Zembla's frost;"

i.e. versatile, able to adapt himself to circumstances.

5.—*Poule.* The old way of spelling Paul; so Chaucer, *Nonne Prests Tale,* 616— "For seint *Poul* saith."

'

Black-jack. A leathern jug for beer. "The large black-jack filled with very small beer of Milnwood's own brewing."—*Old Mortality*, chap. viii.

Seven deadly sins. Pride, Sloth, Gluttony, Lust, Avarice, Envy, and Anger. See the description in Spenser's *Faerie Queene*, bk. i. canto 4.

Sack. A corruption of 'sec,' dry. Falstaff says, "A good sherris-*sack* hath a two-fold operation in it;" and in the same speech speaks of "a second property of your excellent *sherris*." (We have also Canary 'sack,' Malaga 'sack,' inappropriately; for these are sweet, not dry wines; but the word seems to have been considered applicable to all white wines.) So the word came to be used by itself as an equivalent for sherry.

> "*Sack*, says my bush;
> Be merry, and drink *sherry*, that's my posie."
> —BEN JONSON, *New Inn*, i. 2.

Upsees. Generally found in the form 'Upsee Dutch,' or 'Upsee Frise, the Dutch 'op-zyn-fries,' in the Dutch fashion. So Beaumont and Fletcher have 'upsey-English,' in English fashion. "The bowl, which must be 'upsey-English,' strong, lusty London beer." (*Beggar's Bush*, iv. 4.) Scott seems to have mistaken it for a noun.

A fig for the vicar. This expression of contempt is said to be a reminiscence of an ignominious punishment inflicted upon the Milanese by Frederic Barbarossa, in 1162. If a man wished to insult a native of Milan he would remind him of this punishment by putting his thumb between his first and second finger and thrusting it out at him. French 'faire la figue.' (It appears, howevert, to have been also an ancient Italian custom.—DOUCE, *Illustrations of Shakspere*, p. 302.) This action became a common form of insult, or sign of contempt, and the expression is found all over Europe. The same insult was conveyed in another way, by putting the thumb into the mouth. Cp. *Romeo and Juliet*, i. 1: "I will *bite my thumb* at them; which is a disgrace to them if they bear it." Lodge calls it "giving one the *fico*, with his thumb in his mouth." Cp. *Henry V.* iii. 6: "*Fico* for thy friendship."

Placket. (Derivation uncertain.) A petticoat, and so the wearer of a petticoat, in the same way that we speak of petticoat government. Love is called "Dread prince of *plackets*."—*Love's Labour Lost*, iii. 1. So Beaumont and Fletcher, *Hum. Lieut.* iv. 3—

> "Was that brave heart made to pant for a *placket*?"

Pot is used in the same way for the liquor which it contains. This figure is called metonymy, the thing being named by some accompaniment (Greek μετά, ὄνομα); so the *ermine* is put for the judge, or judgeship, the *kettle* for the water in it.

Lurch. The same word as 'lurk,' to lie in wait, to be on the look-out for, sometimes to lie in wait, so as to get a thing first, so to rob. *Coriolanus,* ii. 2—

"He lurcht all swords o' the garland."

A ship *lurches* when it dips, so as to be lost in the trough of the waves.

6. — *Minstrel.* The same word as 'minister.' Provençal 'menestral' = 'artisan.' "Confined in process of time to those who ministered to the amusement of the rich by music and jesting."

Glee-maiden. A necessary attendant of the *jongleur,* or juggler, though she sometimes went about unaccompanied. The readers of the *Fair Maid of Perth* will remember Louise.

Get thee an ape. "The facetious qualities of the ape soon rendered him an acceptable addition to the strolling band of the jongleur. Ben Jonson, in his splenetic introduction to the comedy of *Bartholomew Fair,* is at pains to inform the audience 'that he has ne'er a sword-and-buckler man in his fair, nor a juggler with a well-educated ape, to come over the chain for the King of England, and back again for the Prince, and sit still on his haunches for the Pope and the King of Spain."—SCOTT.

7. — *Purvey.* French 'pourvoir,' to provide. In a royal progress the *purveyors* were those who went before to collect provisions, the sale of which they could enforce, as the *harbinger* secured lodging.

Tartan screen. The tartan served a Scotch maiden as a veil; so of Jeanie Deans: "The want of the screen, which was drawn over the head like a veil, she supplied by a *bon-grace.*"

8. — *Needwood.* Formerly a royal forest in the Trent Valley in Staffordshire.

9. — *Tullibardine* ("the bard's knoll"), near Auchterarder, in Perthshire, an old seat of the Murrays, which was their residence and designation till they acquired the Atholl estates and title by marriage.

Spurs were the natural mark of the 'eques' or knight.

Come ye to seek a champion's aid,
On palfrey white, with harper hoar,
Like errant damosel of yore?

Compare the picture which Spenser gives of Una in the letter to Sir W. Ralegh prefixed to the *Faerie Queene:* "Soone after entred a faire Ladye in mourning weedes, riding on a white Asse, with a dwarfe behind her leading a warlike steed, that bore the armes of a knight, and his speare in the dwarfe's hand. Shee, falling before the Queene of Faeries, complayned that her father and mother had been by a huge dragon many years shut up in a

brazen Castle, and therefore besought the Faery Queene to assygne her some one of her knights to take on him this exployt." Compare also Tennyson's *Gareth and Lynette.*

10.—*Permit I marshal.* An unusual construction; understand 'that.'

Barret-cap. A cloth cap. Italian 'berretta,' French 'barrette,' from Low Latin ' birretum,' and that from ' birrus' or ' byrrhus,' a coarse cloth. The 'berretta' still forms a part of ecclesiastical costume.

11.—*With the Chief's birth,* &c. Note how this speech is framed so as to mislead the hearer. He would naturally suppose the chief to be Roderick.

12.—*Wheel.* An instrument of torture on which malefactors were stretched after their limbs had been broken. Hence the French word 'roué,' ' broken upon the wheel.' Cp.—

"The lifted axe, the agonizing wheel,
Luke's iron crown, and Damiens' bed of steel."
—GOLDSMITH, *Traveller.*

Unhasp. A.S. 'hæps,' 'a latch or bolt of a door ;' German 'haspe.' For the change of letters, compare 'task ' and 'tax.'

Dungeon. An underground prison. The same word as 'donjon,' 'the large tower in a fortress,' 'the keep,' 'that which *commands* the rest.' Latin 'dominio,' 'domnio.' Cp. 'songe,' from 'somnium.'

Garniture; 'furniture,' 'tapestry.' French 'garnir,' Italian 'guarnire,' related to 'garer,' 'to look out,' as our 'warn' (its equivalent), to 'ware.' So it is 'to make another look out,' 'to provide against a thing ;' then 'to provide,' 'furnish.'

Leech. A.S. 'læce,' Gothic 'leikeis,' 'a healer,' 'a physician ;' Icelandic 'lækna,' 'to cure.'

13.—*Prore.* Latin 'prora,' 'prow.'

Stem. To stay, resist. From the root *'sta'* of Greek ἵστημι, Latin 'sto ;' Icelandic 'stemmi.' A ship *stems* the billows by making head against them. Any one who has seen a stranded vessel break up will feel the force of the simile. Nothing gives a better notion of strength made helpless.

14.—*Again where ne'er.* One of Scott's strange inversions for ' where ne'er again.'

O'er Dermid's race. A pibroch of the Macgregor clan celebrated this victory. " There are several instances, at least in tradition, of persons so much attached to particular tunes as to require to hear them on their death-bed."—SCOTT. Brantome gives

a curious instance of a lady at the court of France, who asked to
have played to her in this way a tune composed on the defeat of
the Swiss at Marignano.   The burden of this song was "Tout
est verlore:" "all is lost ;" and when the minstrel came to this
she cried out twice, "Tout est perdu !" and died.

15.—*Battle of Beal' an Duine.*   In 1650 and 1651, after the
battle of Dunbar, Cromwell's troops were occupied in "reducing
detached castles, coercing moss-troopers, and, in detail, bringing
the country to obedience."—CARLYLE'S *Cromwell*, ii. 244.   It
was during this time that "a skirmish actually took place at a
pass thus called in the Trosachs, and closed with the remarkable
incident mentioned in the text."—SCOTT.   One of the soldiers
engaged is buried on a little eminence to the south of the pass.
His death led his comrades to make the attack on the island.
The pass of Bealach an Duine lies considerably above the present road, at the foot of Ben-an.

The liveliness of this description of the battle is due to the
greater variety of the metre, which resembles that of *Marmion.*
The three-accent lines introduced at intervals give it lightness,
and the repetition of the same rhyme enables the poet to throw
together without break all that forms part of one picture.

So lone a lake, so sweet a strand !   A perfect description of
Achray.   Even now, though it is haunted by tourists, if once
you leave their beat, you may get into complete quiet and
solitude ; but it is 'sweet,' not dreary.

Eyry.   A.S. 'æg,' plural 'ægru ;' Old English 'eyren'
(Morris, 96), 'eggs ;' literally 'a collection of eggs,' so 'a nest ;'
generally used only of an eagle's nest. (Greek ὠόν, Latin 'ovum,'
German 'ei.')

Erne ; eagle.   A.S. 'ern' or 'earn,' Gothic 'arn,' German
'aar,' Greek ὄρν-ις, which is supposed to be connected with Stem
ὀρ- of ὄρνυμι, 'to spring.'

Note in this stanza the alliteration which the poet uses in
describing the distant rumbling of the soldiers' march.

16.—*Barbed.*   Used of the trappings of a horse ; probably a
corruption of 'bard,' French 'barde,' 'horse armour.' Cp. A.S.
'barda,' 'an armed war-ship.' Icelandic 'barth,' a beaked ship,
ram.

Battalia.   A plural formed, after a false analogy, like that of
Greek nouns, such as 'phænomenon,' 'idolon.'

Vaward= 'vanward,' 'in the front.' 'Van' is from Italian
'avanti,' French 'avant,' Latin 'ab ante.' Cp. 'vantage' and
French 'avantage.'

17.—*Their flight they ply.*   The meaning of this is not very

clear. Possibly 'they keep up a constant fire,' but they seem in too complete a rout for that. Note the effect of the repeated rhymes.

Twilight wood. Cp. stanza 16 : "A twilight forest frowned." The appearance of the spears and pike was such that in the twilight they might have been mistaken at a distance for a wood.

Serried. French 'serré,' 'closely pressed.' From 'serrer,' Latin 'serare' ('sera'), 'to lock in,' 'bolt,' 'confine.' The doubling of the *r* is a mistake which has arisen from a confusion with 'serra,' 'a saw.'

Tinchel. A snare or gin. "After this there followed nothing but slaughter in this realm, every party ilk one lying in wait for another, as they had been setting *tinchills* for the slaughter of wild beasts."—JAMIESON. It is a sort of *battue*, the game being surrounded and driven together.

18.—*Hurled them.* See v. 8, and note.
Linn. i. 3, and note. "Receives her linn" is receives the waters that form the linn or pool.

19.—*Defile.* A narrow gorge, which must be passed in a *file* or a string ('de' and 'filum,' to string off).

The sun is set, &c. Note the effect of the touch of colour here, and also that of the rhymes within the line.

That parts not but with parting life.
          "The loveliness in death
     That parts not quite with parting breath."—BYRON.

Dirge. Properly 'dirige,' the beginning of a solemn hymn, "Dirige Domine, gressus meos." So Chaucer—
     "Resort, I pray, unto my sepulture,
     To sing my *dirige* with great devocioun."

20.—*Bonnet-pieces.* A gold coin in which the king's head was represented with a bonnet instead of a crown, coined by the "Commons' King."

Duncraggan's widowed dame. See iii. 18.

21.—*Elemental.* Of the elements.

22.—Note the three-fold rhymes.
Requiem (like *dirige*), the first word of the funeral mass in the Romish Church. "Requiem æternam da iis, Domine."

23.—*Storied; i.e.* of painted glass, representing some scene from history.
Fall. Lightened. See v. 3, and note.

24.—*Perch and hood; i.e.* of idleness. The hawk was hooded when it was not to be flown at any game.

Thrall. Confinement. A 'thrall' is a slave (connected by some with A.S. 'thirel,' our 'drill,' the ears of slaves being pierced); hence 'thraldom,' here 'thrall' = 'servitude,' 'captivity.'

Steeple; i.e. of Grey-friars' Church. See v. 20.

Trophies. Prizes of victory. Greek τροπα-ιον, from τροπῆ, a rout.

Prime. Properly the first canonical hour of prayer, 6 A.M. Then applied loosely to the first quarter of the day.

26.—*Presence.* Used in the old poets for the reception-room; so *Henry VIII.* iii. 1, 17—
        "The cardinals wait in the *presence.*"
Romeo and Juliet, v. 3, 86—
        "This vault a feasting *presence* full of light."
Cp. *Marmion,* i. 28—
        "If she had been in *presence* there."

27.—Mr. Ruskin (*Modern Painters,* iii. 248) bids us note the northern love of rocks in the opening of this stanza. "Dante could not have thought of his 'cut rocks' as giving rest even to snow. He must put it on the pine-branches if it is to be at peace." Cp. *Autocrat of the Breakfast Table:* "She melted away from her seat like an image of snow."

Glencairn is the *dowre* enemy of the Douglas in the ballad of *Archie Kilspindie,* quoted on canto v.

28.—*The general eye; i.e.* common, public. Cp. Hamlet's
        "'Twas caviare to the *general.*"
        "*Stirling's tower*
Of yore the name of Snowdoun claims."
"William of Worcester, who wrote about the middle of the fifteenth century, calls Stirling Castle Snowdoun. Sir David Lindsay bestows the same epithet upon it."—SCOTT. The name generally assumed by James V., in his disguise, was the "Laird of Ballingeich," a narrow lane "that leads from the town of Stirling, and descends the precipice behind the castle." He was James (V.), the son of James (IV.).

Talisman. A charm or spell that has magical power to produce some extraordinary effect. From the Arabic 'telsam,' plural 'telsaman,' horoscope; and this from the Greek τετελεσμένα (consecrated), the name given in the Lower Empire to the images of pagan divinities who were deemed mischief-workers.

Conclusion.—Wizard-elm. See introduction to canto i., witch-elm.

GLOSSARIAL INDEX.

GENERAL INDEX TO NOTES.

NEW ELEMENTARY ARITHMETIC ON THE UNITARY METHOD.

By THOMAS KIRKLAND, M.A., Science Master Normal School, and WILLIAM SCOTT, B.A., Head Master Model School, Toronto.

Intended as an Introductory Text-Book to Hamblin Smith's Arithmetic.

Cloth Extra, 176 Pages.   Price 25 Cents.

Highly recommended by the leading Teachers of Ontario.

Adopted in many of the best Schools of Quebec.

Adopted in a number of the Schools of Newfoundland.

Authorized by the Council of Public Instruction, Prince Edward Island.

Authorized by the Council of Public Instruction, Manitoba.

Within one year the 40th thousand has been issued.

ADAM MILLER & Co.,
TORONTO.

www.ingramcontent.com/pod-product-compliance
Lightning Source LLC
Chambersburg PA
CBHW021133020726
47500CB00003B/1051